"Surrender!" Bowspear called ahead. "Surrender, and your lives will be spared!"

"Never!" Trembling with fury, eyes wild and arrogant, the ship's captain appeared in the stern, glaring defiantly down at Bowspear and the longboat.

Bowspear swung the grappling hook, faster and faster, paying out line. With a grunt, he released, and he knew his aim was true.

The *Truda Fey*'s captain leapt forward, sword swinging. He didn't mean to cut the rope, Bowspear realized, but knock the flying grapple back into the water. The captain had badly miscalculated. His thin steel blade shattered like glass against the heavy iron, which sailed past him unstopped.

Jerking the rope, Bowspear snapped the hook around like a whip. Its barbed ends caught the captain's neck and shoulder. The man screamed and tried to free himself, but only tangled himself in the rope. Bowspear heaved with all his might, and the man collapsed, body wedged tight between the deck and the stern railing. His screams became soft gurgles, then stopped altogether. . . .

BOOKS

The Hag's Contract

John Betancourt

THE HAG'S CONTRACT

© 1996 TSR, Inc.
All Rights Reserved.

First Printing: June 1996
Printed in the United States of America.
Library of Congress Catalog Card Number: 95-62208

9 8 7 6 5 4 3 2 1

3114XXX1501

ISBN: 0-7869-0496-8

TSR, Inc.
201 Sheridan Springs Road
Lake Geneva, WI 53147
United States of America

TSR Ltd.
120 Church End, Cherry Hinton
Cambridge CB1 3LB
United Kingdom

To Brian Thomsen,
who always believed in me as a writer.

Dramatis Personae

Albrecht Graben
Although imprisoned in Müden, King Graben continues to rule through his regent, Harlmut the Steward.

Lan Harlmut
King Graben's right-hand man maintains a precarious rule over Grabentod. His loyalty is unquestionable.

Privateer Parniel Bowspear
Bowspear carries the bloodline of a minor awnshegh, which has given him ambitions beyond his station. He has long been prepared to usurp Grabentod's throne . . . and with King Graben imprisoned, his chance may have arrived.

Ythril Candabraxis
This wizard's presence has given Harlmut at least a momentary reprieve, as everyone tries to win his support.

Lady Delma Nauren
King Graben's wife has no interest in politics, but is easily swayed by powerful commoners and pirate captains in the domain.

Haltengabben
This mysterious woman, who runs the thieves guild and the Temple of Ela sees more than she admits.

Captain Terrill Evann
Bowspear's chief rival among the pirate captains of Grabentod is an accomplished swordsman and adventurer. His following is small, but loyal to King Graben.

Captain Evann's Men
Harrach: Evann's right-hand man.
Uwe Taggart: The youngest of the men, at seventeen.
Breitt, Freisch, Lothar, Reddman, Shurdan, Wolfgar, and Turach: Swordsmen and sailors.

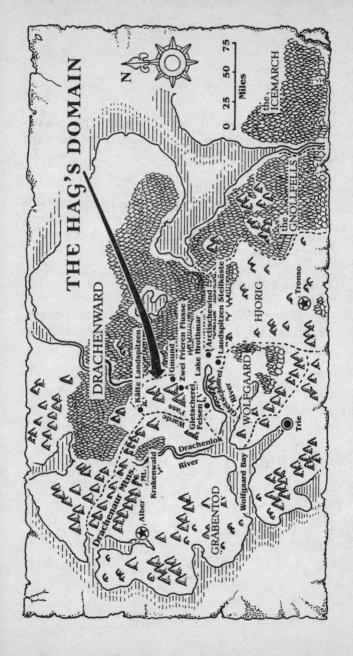

ANUIRE

prologue

In the dark, in a cave high in the Warde Pass, a huge iron cauldron bubbled and frothed over a dimly burning fire, letting loose a fetid stink that would have reminded lesser creatures of death and decay. But not the Hag. She cackled as she worked, tossing in feathers and bits of moss, exotic herbs and colored pebbles, bones and still-warm strips of flesh from creatures her guards had trapped the night before—squirrels, mostly, but also snow hares, a few crows, and even a stray bull moose that had wandered too close to her encampment.

Light suddenly flashed from the cauldron. An eerie glowing mist began to rise from the unholy mixture. Outside, a soft, moaning wind began to howl.

Now, the Hag knew, the time had come.

Leaning forward, she spoke the words of her scrying spell. The glowing mist parted, and she found herself gazing down through the cauldron at a ship on the ocean.

One comes.

She felt a strong source of power on that ship. She had scried upon it thrice in the last two days, and each time it was nearer the rocky shores of Grabentod.

He will be a danger.

She drew in her breath suddenly, knowing her fate was intertwined with the one on that ship. Nothing good would come of their meeting. Blood and fire and death lay in the future. But whose would it be?

He must be killed.

A light step sounded behind her, and suddenly the scrying spell collapsed. It did not matter, the Hag thought. She had seen enough.

She raised her head. The mass of snakes that made up the lower half of her body began to hiss, a sound of recognition rather than fear or anger.

"Pretty-pretty," she said softly, without looking. She combed her long, thin, scraggly white hair with her fingernails. "What news do you bring?"

Orin Hawk, the lieutenant who guarded the northern border of her realm, spoke in a low, powerful voice: "All is ready, Mistress."

She glanced over her shoulder. Hawk's strong blue eyes met hers without hesitation. She saw love and admiration in his gaze, and such devotion as a man would have for his intended bride. Giving a low chuckle, the Hag turned back to her cauldron.

Many years ago, Hawk had been a ranger in the service of the king of Drachenward. He had led a force of thirty men against her. Rather than fight, she had charmed Hawk into her service . . . him and most of his men. Now they worshiped her. They would have died for her, and gladly, had she so commanded. Her bloodline ran deep, all the way back to Azrai the Shadow and the final battle at Mount Deismaar, and she knew the full extent of her powers. Men, she could charm with ease. They were such fools.

But not the one who comes, a tiny voice inside her said. *You cannot charm him.*

He would have to be dealt with more subtly . . . but already her plans were afoot.

"All?" she asked.

"Aye, Mistress."

She chuckled once more. Leaning forward, she caught a faint glimpse of herself reflected in the cauldron, her normally sallow white skin looking green and puckered, the boils and open sores of her face wreathed by the rising steam. Once, she thought, studying her reflection, she had loved gazing into mirrors. That had been a long time ago, back in dim and distant days when she had been human and beautiful. Now she was awnsheghlien, a being of true power. The people of Drachenward and Grabentod might call her an abomination, but she knew better. She was a *power*.

"Good," she said. Yes, every piece of her plot had begun to fall into place. She would kill this newcomer to Grabentod. "We leave at dawn."

"Yes, Mistress," Hawk said.

Aye, them was the days, lad. I seen sixty winters, and my pappy seen sixty-five, so I figure it must've been eighty, ninety years ago when Ulrich Graben sailed into Alber Harbor. He didn't have no fancy titles for him or his men, no Grabentod Raiders, like they call 'em today. In those days, they was just pirates, plain and simple. They lived by their wits and conquered by their swords.

Alber weren't much of a city, then. Maybe five thousand folks lived here, and there weren't much of an army, neither. It was perfect for plundering.

So, like my pappy told it, one winter Captain Ulrich Graben—aye, the great-grandfather of our own king—sailed into the harbor with twelve warships and near a thousand men, and there weren't nobody to stop him. He declared himself the true heir to the Grabentod throne, marched up to the castle like he owned it, kicked open the doors, and that was it. Weren't nobody there to argue. The old regent and all his relatives had run off to the hills, and nobody heard from 'em again. Reckon the goblins or the Hag got 'em.

Anyway, there was King Ulrich Graben, sitting on the throne, and bless him if he didn't get respectable. He set up a proper court, got a bride from Grevesmühl—a noble-born lady, even!—and set about being a king.

That, my fine lad, is how pirates came to rule Grabentod. Now, let me tell ye a real story . . .

ANUIRE

one

"I'll have them!" Parniel Bowspear roared from the longboat's prow. "Pull, there! *Pull!*"

He leaned forward, straining to see through the darkness and fog. Somewhere ahead, he knew, the Müden merchant ship *Truda Fey* lay nearly becalmed, and he intended to have her before daybreak. The *Truda Fey*'s crew had long since doused their lanterns in an effort to hide from him, but it would do them no good. The northern trade winds had failed, and according to Bowspear's reading of the weather signs, they wouldn't resume for another day, at the soonest.

He smiled grimly as his breath plumed in the cold night air. Instead of surrendering to the inevitable, the *Truda Fey*'s captain had played a long cat-and-mouse game with him, bringing his ship close to shore and heading into the fog that perpetually shrouded Grabentod's rocky coastline in the autumn months. Steering through the fog, nursing whatever slight breezes he could catch, always staying just out of reach—that Müden captain had eluded him thus far. But not for much longer, Bowspear thought. He could smell victory. It had come down to a matter of minutes.

"Pull!" he shouted once more to his men. "Pull with all your hearts! *Pull!*"

He felt the longboat surge forward beneath him as the beating drum—already a frantic rhythm—increased its fevered speed. His rowers pulled strongly. If they were tiring, they hadn't shown it yet. Good men, all, he thought proudly. He had handpicked them especially for this mission, selecting from the three units of Grabentod Raiders he commanded. Normally, he would have used a fast sailing ship to capture a merchant vessel like the *Truda Fey*, but with the calm, he'd instead dragged an old longboat from storage. It would more than prove its worth tonight. It could move twice as fast as the *Truda Fey*.

His breath catching in his throat, Bowspear leaned forward, straining to see. There—by King Graben's gray beard, that had to be the merchant's ship!

Slowly, the *Truda Fey* emerged from the gloom and fog. First appeared the broad high stern, painted with the bright emblem of the House of Krael and with Merchant Edom's personal seal. According to Bowspear's spies, the *Truda Fey* carried a rich cargo of silks and spices from Velenoye and Yeninskiy. He meant to have them.

Sucking in a deep breath, he loosened his sword in its scabbard. Only a few more seconds now, he thought, and they would be within striking distance. Müden might hold King Graben prisoner, but that certainly hadn't saved any of their precious cargos. If anything, it had made Bowspear seek out Müden's ships all the more. Of course, he also took ships from Massenmarch, Kiergard, Dauren, and the rest of the domains around the great gulf of the Thaelasian Sea known as the Krakennauricht. Highest of all, though, he prized the ships of Müden's rich merchants.

Actually, he mused, Müden had done him something of a favor in kidnapping King Graben two years back. Once, long ago, he had been a common sailor. When he accidentally slew an awnshegh that attacked his ship north of the Drachenaur Mountains, he found he'd gained the power of its bloodline.

Fortunately there had been no *outward* manifestations of the change—he hadn't been transformed into some hideous monster, like the Hag or the Gorgon. Perhaps that was because the blood of Azrai ran a hundred times stronger in them. Rather, he discovered a craving for power deep inside himself, a craving that could never be quenched by anything short of his own kingdom.

In short, he wanted to rule Grabentod.

Over the last seven years, Parniel Bowspear had worked tirelessly to clear the way for his ascent to the throne. His sudden awnshegh-given fighting prowess had quickly come to the attention of his superiors, and they had awarded him with commission after commission. Now he commanded his own ships and his own raiders.

Of course, he still swore fealty to King Graben, but the day was fast approaching when he would renounce that loyalty and seize the crown for himself. With King Graben imprisoned, the job would be all the easier. The king's steward had done a capable enough job in holding the kingdom together, but his days had just about run out. And with King Graben far away, who could stop Bowspear?

The longboat continued to close with the merchant ship. Bowspear's hand dropped to caress the hilt of his sword, a gift from King Graben himself at the Winter Festival, a scant two months before his capture. With a passion that would have amazed and bewildered lesser men, Bowspear longed to draw that sword, to let it taste blood again.

That passion was another reflection of his altered bloodline, and he tried to control it. But in battle, the awnshegh within took over, driving him into a berserker's frenzy. Even now, he felt that slight slippage in his control beginning. He hoped for the sake of the merchant that no fighting would be necessary.

Only twenty yards to go now, he thought. Muscles in his neck cording like bands of steel, he held himself rigid for a heartbeat, then turned and stalked back along the deck.

"Pull!" he bellowed at his men on their rowing benches. He wanted it over as quickly as possible. "Pull, damn you! I'll have that ship if it breaks your backs! *Pull!*"

Sweat gleamed on their straining bodies, but they bent to the task with a will. The wooden oars creaked; the time-beater pounded his drum like a madman. The longboat leapt ahead.

With a low growl, Bowspear resumed his position in the bow. Already he could see faces ahead, pinpricks of white against the darker wood of the ship as sailors leaned out to peer at him. He threw back his head and roared a wordless challenge into the night. The faces disappeared. Grimly satisfied, he drew back.

The slight wind picked up; with dismay, he watched the *Truda Fey*'s sails fill, and she began to gather speed again, gliding silently ahead. There could be no escape for them this time, Bowspear thought, muttering a quick prayer to the goddess Sera that the calm might resume. His longboat was fast, but no match for the *Truda Fey* under a fair wind.

He cupped one hand to his mouth. "Surrender!" he called ahead. "Surrender, and your lives will be spared!"

"Never!" Trembling with fury, eyes wild and arrogant, the ship's captain appeared in the stern, glaring defiantly down at Bowspear and the longboat.

Despite the sudden breeze, the two ships continued to draw together. They wouldn't escape Bowspear, no matter what they did.

Twenty-five yards, twenty, fifteen—

When ten yards separated the two, Bowspear picked up the spiked iron grappling hook. Behind him, his crewmen still strained at the oars, pulling harder than ever. The rest of his men began to assemble on deck, swords and spears held ready.

Slowly, Bowspear raised the hook and began to swing it over his head, around and around, muscles straining as he played out rope.

Nine yards, eight—

He released the grappling hook. Its line snaked smoothly through his hands, but the hook weighed more than he'd anticipated. It struck too low on the *Truda Fey*'s hull, bouncing harmlessly off and landing in the water. Cursing, Bowspear hauled it back for a second try.

The captain drew his rapier and stood ready, planning, Bowspear knew, to cut the rope if the grappling hook caught.

Six yards, five—

Bowspear began to swing the grappling hook again, faster and faster, paying out line. With a grunt, he released, and this time he knew his aim was true.

The *Truda Fey*'s captain leapt forward, sword

swinging. He didn't mean to cut the rope, Bowspear realized, but knock the flying grapple back into the water. The captain had badly miscalculated. His thin steel blade shattered like glass against the heavy iron, which sailed past him unstopped.

Jerking the rope, Bowspear snapped the hook around like a whip. Its barbed ends caught the captain's neck and shoulder. The man screamed and tried to free himself, but only tangled himself in the rope. Bowspear heaved with all his might, and the man collapsed, body wedged tight between the deck and the stern railing. His screams became soft gurgles, then stopped altogether.

Bowspear heaved a second time. The hook pulled completely through the captain's body and buried itself deep in wood. He heard the man's neck break with a dry, almost wooden snapping sound.

One of the *Truda Fey*'s other officers appeared in the bow. He saw what had happened and ran to finish his captain's task, his long sword sawing at the rope with the sharp steel blade. Strands started to part.

"Bring a harpoon!" Bowspear shouted, dropping his rope to the deck.

His first mate, Bruchen, a tall, fair-skinned man who wore his long blond hair tied behind his head in twin pigtails, came running with a harpoon. Bowspear grabbed it and threw in one continuous blur of motion. It flew straight and hit with a low *thuck*, running straight through the officer's chest.

With a shriek, the man toppled into the sea and vanished from sight.

Three yards—two yards—

"Ship oars!" Bowspear shouted.

A cheer went up among his men as they pulled their oars from the water. Half a dozen Grabentod Raiders ran forward to take Bowspear's grappling line, and others arrived with more hooks, casting them up to the *Truda Fey*. Heaving, in seconds they had the two ships touching, and then they began lashing them together. Now, Bowspear thought, there could be no escape for the merchant ship.

Drawing his short sword, he grasped it between his teeth and pulled himself up the *Truda Fey*'s gunwale. He met no resistance when he swung himself over the railing; the poop deck held only the captain's corpse. He saw no sign of the merchant or any of the ship's other officers. Probably cowering in the hold with their trade goods, he thought with disgust.

He strode to the forward railing and gazed down at the main deck ten feet below. Twenty or so men, mostly common sailors, gazed sullenly up at him. No profits for them this trip.

"Who is in charge here?" Bowspear called.

A dark-haired man in his late twenties stepped forward. He wore a white shirt, green silken vest, dark pantaloons that puffed out at the knees, and a deep red velvet cap with a long red plume. This had to be the merchant, Bowspear thought with contempt.

"I am Edom, merchant of the House of Krael,"

the man announced, smoldering hatred in his eyes. "This is my ship, sir."

Bowspear bowed slightly to him. "An honor, Merchant," he said mockingly. "I am Parniel Bowspear, a privateer of no small consequence in this part of the world."

"Sir," Edom said stiffly. Bowspear could tell it hurt him to address one whom he considered a common thief and pirate so politely. "What is your price?"

"Price? You dare speak of *price* like some passing caravan paying a *border toll?* You are mine, Edom, you and your ship and your crew. *Mine.* Do not forget that."

Edom paled. He clearly wasn't used to being spoken to in such a manner. Müden's merchants had become much too full of themselves of late. Perhaps lessons such as this would help teach them their place in the world.

Müden had lost most of its true nobility in rebellion against Anuirean rule, and in this vacuum, traders and merchants had risen to great power. They prized nothing above money—neither rank nor title nor bloodline. Anyone with sufficient funds could buy the title of merchant, and all of Müden would bow before him. Having bought a title meant little to Bowspear. Now, an earned title, such as privateer, that was a different matter.

"But surely we can reach *some* arrangement?" Edom said with a trace of a whine. "I have silks and spices aplenty aboard—more than enough to assuage your greed, great pirate. I ask only that you leave enough to pay for my voyage and my expenses!"

Bowspear glanced over his shoulder at all his men. Most of them had climbed aboard the *Truda Fey* while he spoke to Merchant Edom.

"What do you think?" he asked. "Shall we leave this fat merchant half his goods?"

They all laughed uproariously at the joke.

Bowspear turned back to Edom and gave a helpless shrug. "I'm sorry, Merchant. My men insist—it's been a bad season, and we're trying to raise a ransom for our king, you know." He gave Edom a wicked grin.

Edom began to tremble with rage, but made no reply.

"I think," said a high, reedy voice, "that half the cargo will be sufficient for your purposes."

Bowspear searched the deck. Who had spoken? He'd hang the fellow up by his thumbs and make an example of him—

Then he spotted a man in dark green robes standing off to one side, watching the scene with interest. He had a long black beard that reached nearly to his belly, a large hooked nose, and piercing blue eyes. Something about those eyes disturbed Bowspear—they seemed to see right into his soul.

"Half," the man in the dark green robes repeated, making a curious motion with one hand, "and no more."

Bowspear grew dizzy. He had to clutch the rail to keep from falling. "Half," he heard himself murmur. Suddenly that seemed like all he needed. He began to nod. "Take half," he said to his men, "and no more. Divide everything in the holds equally."

"Sir," Bruchen said, sounding puzzled, "why take half when we can have it all?"

"Obey my orders!" Bowspear roared, turning on him, fist upraised to strike. He would not tolerate arguments from his men. He'd given his orders; they would obey, or he'd slit their throats himself!

Bruchen did not flinch, and Bowspear gave him credit for that. Any other man on the longboat would have. He knew they feared him, and rightfully so.

"Aye, sir," Bruchen said. He gave the order, and most of Bowspear's men headed for the cargo holds.

"Get my bags, too," the man in the green robes said. "I would like to see your pirate kingdom, Parniel Bowspear. You will bring me ashore."

"Get his bags," Bowspear heard himself saying. He wondered at the words—it seemed so unlike him, even to himself. "Snap to it!"

TWO

Ythril Candabraxis pulled up the hem of his robes and allowed Parniel Bowspear to take his elbow and help him down the gangplank to the longboat.

The spell of charming seemed to be holding remarkably well, considering the inner turmoil the mage now sensed in Bowspear. The pirate captain apparently carried traces of an old and powerful bloodline, and so could fight against the spell on some inner level. Lesser men would merely have surrendered their wills completely.

Candabraxis could barely believe what he'd just done. Was he mad, getting off in Grabentod? A week before, he had booked passage on the *Truda Fey* in Velenoye, a small holding on the northeastern coast of Cerilia, and his destination had originally been Müden. Following the end of his journeyman's contract, he had decided to see the world and set about making his name and fortune. He'd thought Müden, with its rich merchants, would be a good place to look for a patron, but as they'd sailed past Grabentod's rocky shores, he'd found himself staring inland more and more. Some inner sense spoke to him about this place. He couldn't say why, exactly, but he felt some flicker of recognition, a sense of déjà vu, and he had slowly come to realize that his destiny might, in fact, lie here.

The strange calm that left them all but stranded off Grabentod's coast for the previous day merely added to his convictions. It had happened *too* conveniently. His old master had taught him that nothing in this world happened by accident, so after a long chase through the fog, when the pirates had finally taken the ship, he had decided to follow his impulses and accompany the pirates back to Grabentod. Perhaps, he thought, he would discover more about this kingdom and how it came to be so . . . familiar to him.

Bowspear personally carried the mage's bags to the low cabin in the stern of the longboat. Candabraxis thought he might have overdone things a bit when he noticed how the other pirates stared and muttered among themselves. Still, they seemed to fear their captain, for none of them spoke openly of his odd behavior. Besides, the spell lasted only a day; he'd be back to his old gruff self tomorrow.

"Thank you," he said as the pirate set his bags by the door. He turned up the wick of the oil lantern. A clear yellow light filled the cabin, revealing a single bunk, a chart table, and a rack of three swords by the door. Austere at best, he decided, much like the quarters of a wizard's journeyman. He smiled. Yes, he thought, this cabin would do quite well until they made it back to port.

He turned to the pirate captain. In the light, Bowspear looked younger than Candabraxis had first thought, no more than thirty. His face, lined and creased from years spent in the open and under the sun, made a sharp contrast to his neatly groomed mustache and short brown hair. His hardened leather shirt and the short sword at his side looked expensive and well cared for. Clearly he was a man used to the best of all things.

"Let me get you a drink." Bowspear fetched clay cups from a cabinet and poured them both liberal servings of a dark red wine.

Candabraxis sipped and found it excellent—a dry Anuirean summer wine. The full, rich taste gave it away. It had probably been destined for the table of one of Müden's merchant-princes before being appropriated by Grabentod's pirates. He'd seldom tasted its equal.

Bowspear went on, "Is there anything else you need?"

"How long will the trip back to Grabentod take?"

"Four hours, perhaps five." He gave a shrug. "The men are tired. It's been a long night. Now that we have our cargo, there is no need to hurry."

Five hours . . . Candabraxis nodded. He could finish his sleep, he realized, and arrive refreshed.

"That will do nicely," he said. He drained the rest of the wine, handed the cup back to Bowspear, then stretched out on the bunk. The pallet was harder than he'd expected, but it would do. "Return to the deck and keep watch. Wake me when we're in sight of your port . . . what's its name?"

"Alber."

Alber. He wondered what it would be like.

* * * * *

Candabraxis came awake with a start and found Bowspear looming over him. The pirate's face was grim. The spell of charming had started to wear off, the wizard realized. Bowspear had begun to wonder why he was being so kind to this stranger, but had yet to realize kindness wasn't necessary. Hopefully it would last long enough to see them safely ashore. Although he could always cast the spell again, he didn't want to—if he ended up staying in Grabentod, it had to be on an honest footing. Few people trusted wizards, and none trusted a wizard who kept those in power charmed against their wills.

"We're approaching Alber," Bowspear said.

Sitting up, Candabraxis gave him a quick nod. "Good. I'll join you on deck."

Together they stepped out into the brightness of late morning. The drummer beat a steady rhythm, and rowers pulled strongly at the oars. Shivering, Candabraxis pulled his belt a little tighter, glad he'd worn his heaviest robes for the journey. The chill wind had picked up, and it carried a razor's edge this morning. He'd always heard that winters in this part of the world could be hard, and for autumn it seemed far colder than it should have been. No wonder ice sheets closed the local harbors when true winter fell.

Shading his eyes, he turned to the east and squinted. The sun had already driven off the night's fog, and now he could clearly see the jagged, rocky coast of Grabentod. The longboat angled toward a natural inlet with steep cliffs rising fifty or sixty feet high to either side. Ahead, somewhere beyond the cliffs, he could make out two stone towers jutting above the land, and the dark smudges of hundreds of cooking fires rose wraithlike into the clear blue sky.

In the far, far distance rose the mist-shrouded Drachenaur Mountains. Rumor said half a dozen dragons lived there. For a second, the wizard squinted at their snow-capped peaks, but no trace of movement caught his eye. Some people believed spotting a dragon meant ill fortune to come, although he put no store in such old wives' tales. He would have welcomed such an exhilarating spectacle. He had, after all, set out to see the world.

Bowspear headed for the prow of the longboat, walking with a slight rolling gait that compensated for the longboat's surging movement, and Candabraxis followed, steadying himself on the deck rails. From here, as the longboat rounded a curve, he had a magnificent view of the city ahead. He counted ten long piers stretching like fingers out into the natural harbor, and a number of sailing vessels lay moored there.

His gaze swept ashore. Long, low warehouses sat just inland, and beyond them, crawling up the slope of a hill, lay Alber proper: hundreds of stone houses with thatched or red tiled roofs, forming a maze of narrow cobblestone streets. On the highest hill, perhaps a quarter of a mile above the water, sprawled a large stone castle with ramparts and the two watchtowers he'd spotted earlier. From such vantage points, Candabraxis thought, the pirates of Grabentod could doubtless spot ships far out to sea. Perhaps that was how they'd learned of the *Truda Fey*.

He turned and found Bowspear once more scowling at him. "You—" the pirate began.

"Please, forgive me," Candabraxis said, spreading his arms apologetically. "It was a minor charm, and one of no lasting effect. At the time, I thought it necessary to safeguard my passage. I wanted to return to Grabentod with you, and I feared you might refuse."

"Why?" Bowspear demanded, eyes narrowed to slits. "You could have escaped with your merchant friend Edom. Why come here? And why save only half his cargo?"

Candabraxis sighed and leaned on the rail. "Young Edom is a fool, but he did me a few small kindnesses along the journey. This was his first trading voyage. He had invested his entire fortune in his cargo. Had you taken it all, you would have ruined him. Now, he will have profits enough to reinvest and, should he meet with success, you will have more of his cargos to plunder in future seasons."

The pirate pursed his lips, but nodded slowly. "Very well, I accept that answer. But why come to Grabentod? Why not sail on to Müden?"

"Perhaps . . ." Candabraxis hesitated. "I don't really know," he admitted. "I had a feeling, when I saw this place, that my destiny must somehow lie here." He turned to gaze inland and found a lump in his throat. "I cannot explain it. I have never felt anything so strongly before in my life. I *had* to come."

"We have no wizard," Bowspear said, regarding him carefully. "It's something the king has tried to remedy for years."

"Then perhaps I am meant to be that wizard."

"There are other powers at work in Grabentod," Bowspear said, still studying him, though now his look had grown calculating. "You would do well to choose friends carefully here, Wizard."

Clearly, Bowspear intended that as a warning of

some kind. Could a power struggle be going on in Grabentod? If so, he would have to watch his step.

"Friends . . . like you?" he asked tentatively.

"I'm the most successful captain in the fleet. My fortunes are rising. I would make a powerful ally for anyone looking to Grabentod's future."

"And where do you place your allegiance?" Candabraxis asked slowly. "With King Graben?"

The rowers had begun dragging their oars in the water to slow the longboat as they coasted up to the piers. Bowspear called a few orders to his men, who pulled ropes from lockers and prepared to moor the longboat.

Done, Bowspear turned and smiled. It was the look of a predator, Candabraxis thought.

"I *am* one of King Graben's sworn men, of course. He is our ruler. If he were here instead of held prisoner in Müden, he would be ruler in more than just name."

"But he's not here."

"No. His steward, Harlmut, rules in his name."

Bowspear offered nothing else, and Candabraxis did not pry. By the very nature of their powers, wizards often found themselves embroiled in politics, and he had the distinct feeling a palace coup lay in Grabentod's future.

The rowers began shipping their oars. Other sailors dropped fenders off the starboard side of the longboat as it bumped alongside the second pier from the left, and then they began lashing it fast. Bowspear leapt nimbly from the prow to the deck.

Candabraxis chose to walk back to the gang-plank sailors had dropped into position. One of many lessons his old master had taught him had been: A wizard must be dignified at all times. Had he tried to follow Bowspear and fallen into the sea, he never would have lived it down. Nick-names like "Candabraxis the Soggy" or "Candabraxis the Clumsy" would have been the least of it.

"Start bringing the cargo ashore," Bowspear called to his first mate. "Start a tally. I'm off to see Harlmut and let him know we met with success. We'll divide shares tonight. When you're done, three rounds at Blind Melior's for everyone—on me!"

A cheer rose from the crew.

Bowspear grinned. "A good night's work, lads!" he called.

Candabraxis joined him. He, too, needed to see the king's steward. It would be interesting to meet the man King Graben trusted with his kingdom.

"This way." Bowspear turned and started up the road toward the castle.

three

From the east watchtower, Harlmut the Steward gazed down at the city he ruled in King Graben's name and wondered what it would be like to live here under Parniel Bowspear's rule. Not much different, he thought. The lives of the twenty thousand men, women, and children who lived in the city surrounding Castle Graben would scarcely be affected. The weavers would be busy for a season or two, putting Bowspear's face on all the tapestries and wall-hangings, and the cooks would enjoy a few more celebratory feasts than usual. Of course, some people—himself included—would quietly disappear. Otherwise . . .

He sighed. It had all become a matter of time. These days he spent his hours watching, waiting, and trying to hold on to power as Parniel Bowspear deftly forged secret alliances designed to win him the throne. The king's last few loyal spies had just brought word of secret agreements with Haltengabben, the woman who controlled the Night Walkers and the Temple of Ela. If she backed Bowspear openly, most of the king's men would follow. And why not? King Graben had been gone nearly two years now. These people wanted a stronger hand than he could provide. The best he could hope for would be maintaining the status quo until he found some way to ransom King Graben back or the king escaped on his own.

The wind ruffled Harlmut's long gray hair, and he swept it back with one hand. How he longed for the simpler days, when King Graben himself sat on the throne and made the decisions. Back then he had enjoyed his work. As steward, his only duties had been to keep the castle's household running, manage the stores and provisions, and keep King Graben's schedule. Now, acting in the king's name, he did all that and more.

Although nearly sixty, Harlmut had the keen eyesight of a man a third his age. Leaning his elbows on the parapet, he studied the longboat that had just pulled up to the docks below. He had thought Bowspear mad when he'd dragged an old longboat, of all things, from one of the storage sheds, but the mission's success spoke volumes about the correctness of that decision. Harlmut had half hoped Bowspear would return empty-handed. It might have forestalled the conflict to come. Now, flushed with his recent successes, Bowspear could move as quickly as he wanted. The end would almost certainly come within half a month.

A bearded man in long green robes got off the longboat. Harlmut drew in a sudden breath and leaned out another foot, straining to see. A hostage . . . or a passenger? He squinted. Bowspear didn't seem to be treating the stranger like a prisoner. He seemed almost . . . deferential. Why?

It could mean only more trouble for the king. Frowning, Harlmut stood and straightened his heavy black and gold tunic, brushing dust from his elbows. Bowspear and the stranger had started up the road toward Castle Graben. Harlmut turned to go. He would have to be in the king's audience hall when they arrived.

* * * * *

Bowspear provided the wizard with a running commentary on the city of Alber and the kingdom of Grabentod as they walked up the narrow dirt road toward the castle, but Candabraxis only half listened. The pirate captain was trying too hard to be pleasant and likable. Clearly the wizard had arrived at a time when his presence might tip the balance in some power struggle, and Bowspear hoped to win his support. The more time they spent together, though, the less Candabraxis liked the pirate captain.

". . . almost eighty years ago, Ulrich Graben, a great warrior, led a fleet from the Zweilunds and settled his people here," Bowspear was saying. "I can trace my own family back to Antilen Bowspear, who served as his first officer. . . ."

The wizard felt little interest in local politics. He had a larger and vastly more interesting puzzle before him. Grabentod still seemed all too familiar. *How?* How could he possibly know this place if he had never set foot here before? He'd heard ancient tales of reincarnation, but no wizard worthy of the name paid much attention to them. And yet . . . the buildings, the faces, the very streets cried out in silent recognition. He had been here before. Somehow, in some way, he had been here before.

". . . and some say Ulrich made an unholy pact with the Hag for the power to free his land from orog and goblin tribes," Bowspear said, "but I don't put much store by that, myself. Now—"

"The Hag?" Candabraxis interrupted, frowning. "Ah yes, a minor awnshegh. I've read of her."

She had a rather bizarre history, as he recalled. She had originally come from this area, long before it had been called Grabentod, and she'd married into the Drachenward royal family. Following the death of her husband, she had been sent home in disgrace. Before she left, though, she kidnapped a young girl, the heir to the Drachenward throne.

After that, even her homeland would have none of her. She had eventually fled into the mountains, and there she had gradually changed into the Hag, as her true evil nature and her bloodline asserted themselves. The neighboring nations had been at war ever since, sometimes openly and sometimes not.

"There's nothing minor about the Hag," Bowspear said, making a sign of aversion. "Everyone here has been touched by her evil in some way."

"Oh? Does she bother Grabentod much?" he asked.

"We've heard nothing of her in nearly a year," Bowspear said, "thanks be to Neira. Now, as I was saying, Castle Graben was built fifty years ago on the foundations of the old castle, when the old king brought in stonemasons from Aulbrunn . . ."

They were nearly to the castle's gates. A pair of pikemen snapped to attention, and Bowspear gave them a casual salute without missing a word in his history lecture. Through the gates, they passed into a large courtyard paved with red and green flagstones. Huge double doors led into a large hall directly in front of them; stables stood far to the right and, to the left, sat a large smithy. Steel clanged on steel as the blacksmith, a tall barrel-chested man with a chestnut beard and a huge leather apron, worked on horseshoes with several apprentices.

"The king's steward is named Lan Harlmut," Bowspear said, heading for the main hall. Apparently the history lecture was over. "He's a fair enough man, but lacking in vision."

"Surely that's one of the characteristics of a good regent," Candabraxis commented dryly. "A greater man, or a lesser one, might well have designs on this kingdom."

Bowspear shot him a strange look, as though uncertain how to take that.

Good, Candabraxis thought smugly. Let him worry. This Harlmut the Steward sounded more and more like the sort of man who deserved his support.

* * * * *

Harlmut sat patiently on the king's high, stone throne, waiting for Bowspear and the man in green robes to appear. He had never felt entirely at ease sitting here, in the audience chamber, but it came with the job. He stared at the rich tapestries hanging on the walls, studied the amber flames licking at the logs in the huge fireplace to his left, and felt a creeping depression at what would come next.

Half a dozen commoners had been standing off to one side, patiently awaiting the chance to have an audience with him. He gave a quick nod to the guard, who escorted the first two—a pair of common sailors—to stand before him. Might as well get it over with, he thought.

He pulled himself up to his fullest height. "What brings you before me?" he demanded, trying his best to sound authoritative.

"Sir . . ." said the first, and he launched into a convoluted tale, interrupted frequently with embellishments by the second, of how they'd both seen a small trunk washed up on shore. Now each one wanted to claim it for himself.

Greed, Harlmut reflected, seemed to motivate everyone around him. The trunk had undoubtedly been dumped overboard by a merchant ship to prevent its being taken by the Grabentod Raiders. This sort of thing happened once or twice a year. It was the Grabentod Raiders' standard procedure to burn ships they caught playing such tricks, so it happened less and less.

"What did you find in the trunk?" he asked, imagining silks, rare spices, or jewelry.

The two glanced at each other. "We ain't opened it yet," the first one admitted. They were probably afraid it would lead to bloodshed, Harlmut realized, and so they were trying to resolve ownership beforehand.

"Why not divide the contents between you?" he asked.

"What if there's only one thing of value?" the second said. "Seems to me, since I saw it first—"

"*I* saw it first," the other said sharply.

"Silence!" Harlmut shouted. Disputes such as this one sapped his patience and his strength. He didn't know how King Graben managed to hold court year after year without going mad. Already he felt a severe headache beginning to develop. "Where is the trunk now?" he demanded.

"Outside," the first sailor said, cowed, "with your guards."

"Very well," Harlmut said, "I have made my decision. The chest is to be opened in the courtyard by one of the king's men. Because you could not settle this matter yourselves, half the contents are forfeit to King Graben. The other half will be divided equally between you. If it's a single item of value, as you suspect, you will be compensated from the royal treasury for your shares."

"But—" the second one began, with a shocked look on his face.

"That's my decision," Harlmut snapped. "Would you rather the royal treasury confiscate the whole trunk and all its treasure?"

"N-No sir!"

"Then get out of my sight, and don't bring trivialities to me again!"

Bowing, they hastily backed away. The guard escorted them out.

They had looks of actual *fear* on their faces, Harlmut thought, a little awed at himself. He seldom spoke to anyone in such tones. Today, with everything unraveling about him, he couldn't muster the patience to deal with petty bickering. Perhaps some good would come of it, though. Next time, they'd try to settle matters themselves rather than lose half of their disputed treasure to the king.

Frowning, Harlmut turned his gaze to the other four supplicants waiting to see him.

"Who's next?" he demanded.

The following pair in line—more sailors—muttered excuses and edged toward the door. The two shopkeepers waiting behind them followed suit. A dozen heartbeats later, Harlmut sat alone, with just the guards by the door and a few servants sweeping the floor. Just as well, he thought. If he had a confrontation with Parniel Bowspear coming, he would be better off facing it alone. Enough rumors surrounded him already, without commoners carrying more back to Alber's taverns.

Suddenly the main doors flew open and Bowspear swaggered in with a wide, triumphant grin on his face. That grin always meant trouble. Harlmut shifted uncomfortably on the throne and tried to look more confident than he felt.

"I take it you met with success," the king's steward said.

"That we did, Harlmut." Bowspear had made it a habit never to address him as "regent" or "sir." It was a deliberate slight, Harlmut knew, but he always let it pass. Fight the battles you can win, King Graben had always said. "We took a rich merchant's cargo as prize. I will be dividing shares tonight, if you want to come."

"No need," Harlmut said. "As a sworn king's man, I know you'll do your duty by the royal tithe." He swept his gaze up and beyond Bowspear to the bearded stranger, as if noticing him for the first time. "I see you brought a guest back with you."

"Aye," Bowspear said, and his grin grew larger, if that were possible. This man had to be truly dangerous, Harlmut realized. "I want you to meet a friend, a powerful wizard from Velenoye."

A wizard, Harlmut thought, and he tried to stifle his surprise. No wonder Bowspear felt so cocky. With a wizard backing his grab for power . . .

"From Suiriene, actually," the wizard said, stepping forward and bowing low to Harlmut. His voice was far softer than Harlmut had expected. "I came by way of Velenoye, where I spent my apprenticeship and journeyman years. My name is Ythril Candabraxis. I am honored to be here, Regent Harlmut."

"As we are honored to have you as our guest, Candabraxis." Harlmut studied him thoughtfully. Candabraxis seemed young and a trifle hesitant for a wizard. The few whom Harlmut had interviewed, trying to persuade them to take up residence in Grabentod, had struck him as egotistical and self-important. Perhaps Candabraxis would not prove quite so dangerous after all.

"What brings you to our kingdom?" he asked.

The wizard told him sketchily of his first sight of Grabentod and how it had stirred memories within him. He had come, he said, to learn what had called him here.

Harlmut nodded, intrigued. "You have no definite plans here, then?" he asked, leaning forward. Bowspear had begun to look faintly uneasy. "You had not meant to come to our shores?"

"No," Candabraxis said firmly. "I was bound for Müden in hopes of finding a patron."

"Then you must, of course, stay in the castle while you investigate. Winter is coming, and the seas will soon be closed to ships. We have a suite in the northern tower. I'm told it would be ideal for a wizard. I'm certain that spending the winter months here is more advisable than continuing on to Müden."

Candabraxis nodded. "Yes . . . I think I would like that, Regent. I am indebted for your hospitality."

Harlmut deigned to notice the displeased glances Bowspear had been giving Candabraxis.

"Are you ill, Captain?" he asked.

"Yes," Bowspear said through clenched teeth.

"You're not looking well," Candabraxis said, turning to face him. "If you'd like, I would be happy to try another spell . . . ?"

"That won't be necessary," Bowspear said stiffly.

"It's no great effort, I assure you," the wizard said with a smile.

"No," Bowspear said, more strongly.

"Perhaps you should take your leave of us now, Captain," Harlmut said, rising. He gazed down at Bowspear and felt a new confidence. "I believe you have shares to divide up? I will see to settling Wizard Candabraxis into his suite. After we have tea, of course."

"My men won't have finished unloading yet," Bowspear protested.

"Then why don't you see what's holding them up," Harlmut said, stepping down and taking the wizard's elbow. "I will proclaim a feast in Candabraxis's honor. You *will* attend, of course, Captain." He deliberately made it a statement rather than a question.

"Of course," Bowspear said curtly.

"There is still the matter of my baggage," Candabraxis began hesitantly. "If I'm to stay here—"

"Captain Bowspear will see to it."

"I'll have it brought here," Bowspear said.

"Good." Harlmut gently steered Candabraxis toward one of the smaller rooms at the back of the main hall. He felt a flash of triumph. This was the first time he'd had the last word with Bowspear in months. Now he and the wizard could have a quiet chat.

He opened a door into the room that had been King Graben's private office. The walls had been paneled with Grabentod oak, and hunting trophies—the heads of deer, elk, and other animals—hung beside military banners, swords, shields, and other spoils of war. A heavy oak desk to one side held papers—cargo manifests, land grants, and other business Harlmut worked on late at night. Thank goodness he had never married, he thought, or there wouldn't have been enough hours in the day.

"Please," he murmured to Candabraxis, gesturing toward one of the two deep, comfortable chairs beside the fieldstone fireplace. He stirred the logs with a poker, and soon amber flames rose. Once the wizard had seated himself, he said, "I prefer tea in the winter months, but you might prefer something else. We have warm spiced ale, mulled apple cider—"

"Tea is fine," Candabraxis said.

Harlmut rang a bell, and a second later a boy appeared in the doorway. He ordered their drinks, then joined the wizard by the fire.

"About Captain Bowspear . . ." Candabraxis began.

Harlmut sighed. Already it came to that. The tension between the two of them would have been palpable to one as well trained and powerful as a wizard. No doubt Candabraxis had already sized up the situation and guessed the problems Harlmut faced.

"Yes," he said, nodding. "There is no love between us, as I'm sure you noticed. Just as you no doubt already know that King Graben is a prisoner of Müden's royal marines."

"And that Bowspear wants to be king."

"He said that?" Harlmut leaned forward eagerly. If so, and if Candabraxis would act as witness, he could arrest Bowspear for treason. Bowspear had always been careful with his plans in the past, but if he'd made a mistake here—

Candabraxis was shaking his head, though. "No, but I could see it easily enough. He is a man of great ambition."

"And greater luck." Harlmut sank back into the other chair. "He is by far the most successful of Grabentod's Raiders. And his men—and half the city—worship him."

"I remain curious, though. It seems to me that

this whole situation could be resolved with King Graben's return."

"True," Harlmut said, nodding.

"And according to Bowspear, you're completely loyal to King Graben. So why haven't you ransomed your king back?"

"Do you think I haven't tried?" Harlmut forced a laugh. "Müden doesn't want our money. They could buy and sell all of Grabentod from their household accounts without noticing. What they want is safe passage for their ships."

"Yet clearly they don't have it."

"No." The steward shrugged helplessly. "We simply cannot afford to give Müden safe passage. Our economy is based on raiding—it would collapse without it. I cannot allow our people to starve. As you can see, it is a difficult situation."

"I'm sure Müden feels the same way. But surely something can be done. Have you explored other options?"

"Exhaustively." Harlmut sighed and shook his head. He'd spent the first year of King Graben's imprisonment sending proposal after proposal to Müden. All had been rebuffed. "No success."

"Perhaps you could trade someone for him. . . ."

"I've thought of that, too," Harlmut said. "None of Müden's important merchant princes are careless enough to venture within reach of our ships. Hired captains, young nobles, those we catch aplenty—and all the while Müden's ruling merchants sit in their palaces and count their money."

"Still," the wizard mused, "there must be *someone*.

Müden's bloodlines have connections far across Cerilia. Perhaps another suitable person can be found. I have a copy of *Morweit's Peerage*. I will study the problem for you and let you know what I find."

"Then you truly will remain in the castle as my guest?"

The wizard chuckled, a light and pleasant sound to Harlmut's ears. "What you mean to ask," Candabraxis said, "is whether I've accepted Bowspear's patronage."

"Since you put it so bluntly—yes."

"And I will be equally blunt. No, I have not accepted his patronage. But I do not think I will accept your king's yet, either. At least, not until I meet him."

Harlmut's shoulders sank. "That may be a wise move," he admitted. "According to my few loyal spies, Bowspear planned to seize power in the coming week. I could not have stopped him."

"He will not try," Candabraxis promised. Despite his soft voice and polite manners, Candabraxis was a man of deep morality, Harlmut saw. "At least, not while my loyalties are in doubt."

Harlmut raised his eyes to meet the wizard's gaze. The regent recognized a deep strength of character there, a sense of justice and propriety that mirrored his own. But such impressions were, perhaps, too fleeting to weigh in the balance against the ambitious pirate. Bowspear had been working toward his coup for years now.

"I wish I could be sure," he murmured.

ANUIRE

four

Parniel Bowspear felt like smashing something.
As he stomped from Castle Graben and descended the long road toward the docks, a rage like none he'd ever felt before washed over him. He could have wrung that wizard's neck—and Harlmut's, too, while he was at it.

Candabraxis and Harlmut had taken one look at each other and gotten as cozy as old friends. Now the two of them would be drinking and joking together, laughing at what a fool they'd made of him. He scowled.

How easily he'd been charmed, he thought. He'd have to make sure it didn't happen again. Surely someone in Grabentod could provide him with a protective amulet or talisman of some sort. . . .

Taking a series of deep breaths, he forced the white-hot rage to cool. The wizard's presence changed nothing. Wizard or no wizard, Grabentod would be his. It just might take a little longer.

He felt light fingers on his belt and whirled, one hand dropping to the hilt of his sword. The thieves guild might be small in Grabentod, but it existed, and he knew the touch of a cutpurse when he felt it.

He found a dirty-faced boy of perhaps eight or ten standing there and looking solemnly up at him. Some street urchin, he thought. He felt no pity or sympathy; life was hard, and it was about to get harder for this little would-be thief. Hard faced, he drew his short sword. He'd give the boy a scare he wouldn't soon forget.

Then he realized the boy wasn't holding anything. Bowspear felt his purse and found it right where it belonged. And something extra seemed to be inside it.

"From Haltengabben." The boy grinned suddenly, then turned and dashed up a narrow alleyway.

Haltengabben. It translated roughly as "Stand and Deliver" . . . the name used by the woman who ran the Temple of Ela and, through it, the thieves guild. Over the last month, he had met with her half a dozen times. She had wanted assurances that, should his fortunes change suddenly for the better, her place in Grabentod would remain secure. Of course it would, he'd said with a cool smile. He'd never had much sympathy for the thieves guild—after all, he did the same work, but openly and respectably—but he recognized the importance of its support. He would need the guild's favor to keep the crown.

Bowspear glanced around. A few old women talking on the corner had turned to stare at him, so he resheathed his sword and resumed his walk. Idly, as if reaching for a sweet, he removed the small pebble the boy had placed in his pouch.

White. That meant she wanted to meet with him again. What could she want now? They'd settled everything last week, or so he'd thought.

After a moment's hesitation, he turned right and headed for the Temple of Ela, on the far side of Alber. Haltengabben hid her illegal activities behind the temple's facade of respectability. It was an open secret, of course, but she kept up pretenses, nonetheless.

He crossed into the old section of the city. Here the stone houses stood shoulder to shoulder, leaning far over the crazy, unplanned hodgepodge of blind alleys and switchback streets. As always, Old Town bustled with life. Dogs barked and chickens scratched in the street; women headed to the market or swept the cobblestones clean in front of their houses; a few old sailors sat on stools in the shade, sipping ale and trading lies; a ragtag mob of children ran past, screaming and laughing, caught up in some game.

A couple of the old sailors stopped their yarns to call greetings to Bowspear. His presence seemed to be causing something of a stir, he reflected. With forced cheerfulness, he waved to the sailors. Few enough high-placed people came to Old Town, and then usually in secrecy and darkness, to visit the Night Walkers.

Now, as more and more faces peered at him from curtained windows, as people on the street turned to stare, he quickened his step. He'd been here too often, he thought, and they had no doubt spent many long hours speculating on his visits to see Haltengabben.

At last he reached the imposing Temple of Ela, a huge stone building set well back from the street. It took up half of a block all by itself, with tall narrow windows set high up on its walls and equally impressive oak double doors. Allowing himself not a second's hesitation, Bowspear strode up the broad steps and into the entry hall.

Two smoking braziers stood to either side of the doorway, and incense spiced the air. Somewhere ahead, deeper in the temple, he heard the *ching-ching-ching* of small cymbals and the frantic strumming of an eight-stringed lute. He paused a second, listening and peering around in the dimness. Someone had met him here every other time he'd come, but today he found himself alone.

He moved forward slowly, rounding the large marble statue of a beautiful woman—the goddess

Ela—with her arms outstretched as if in supplication. She was the patron goddess of thieves and prostitutes and those who worked the darker professions; like his men, Bowspear preferred Sera, the goddess of the sea.

The music grew louder as he stepped through the doorway to the temple's main hall. Bowspear drew up short, staring.

Half a dozen men and women dressed in loose black clothing danced with wild abandon around the altar stone. He felt the hair on the back of his neck beginning to prickle in fear. The dancers' arms rose and fell as they gyrated; their heads whipped around; their hair lashed. Still the cymbals *ching-chinged* and the lute played, the melody pulsing like a heartbeat.

On the altar, movement caught his eye. A huge serpent lounged there. It had to be forty feet long. Languidly it raised its head, tasting the air with its forked tongue, and when it turned toward him, its eyes began to glow with ruby light.

Bowspear found himself transfixed by its gaze. He couldn't move, couldn't breathe. He heard blood thundering in his ears. Then slowly, like a flower unfurling its petals one by one, a coldness began to bloom in his chest.

He found himself floating away from his body, and his consciousness took in the whole of the room. He noticed, in every corner, huge brass braziers filled with burning coal. From them rose a dense black smoke that writhed in time to the movements of the dancers. It seemed to him, then, that the snake and the smoke and the dancers were all a single part of some larger being.

Abruptly the snake lowered its head and hissed at him, and suddenly he found he could move again. He stumbled backward, making a quick sign to avert evil, then turned and fled.

What in Sera's name had he seen inside? Some dark, unholy magic, an inner voice said. Something he didn't want to see again.

Reaching the street, he ran. From somewhere behind him he heard a wild cackle of laughter, but he couldn't tell whether it came from Haltengabben, one of her subjects, or something not quite of this world.

* * * * *

Haltengabben finished the Harvest Ritual, then passed around a bowl of ceremonial white wine. The dancers, drenched with sweat, panting for breath, paused to sip long and hard.

"Dismissed," she said, waving them away.

Rising, they trotted into the back of the temple. They would bathe, change into fresh clothing, and retire until the early evening. Then their work would begin. Bowspear had brought in a new shipload of loot, and she would take the temple's share that very night, under the cover of darkness.

She sighed as she thought of the ruined ceremony. Bowspear's gesture of aversion—done so quickly and thoughtlessly—had set the spells off track. Nevertheless, she placed no blame on him.

The real fault had been hers: she never should have sent for him until after the Harvest Ritual had reached its conclusion. She hadn't expected him back from his meeting with Harlmut so soon.

Rising, she trailed the serpent into the back part of the temple. She found the creature coiled in her office, before her desk. It held its head level with her own. Its ruby eyes glinted as it stared at her, and slowly it began to sway back and forth, making a low crooning sound deep in its throat.

"None of those tricks," she said sharply. "Ela protects me from such charms."

The serpent hissed sharply: a laugh. Then, with the Hag's voice, it said, "So true, my pretty. At least so far."

"What do you want?" She moved a pile of scrolls from her chair onto her equally cluttered desk. The serpent had appeared in the middle of the Harvest Ritual, but had made no interruptions until it finished.

"A ship has come, and on that ship there rode a man in green. I want him dead."

Haltengabben blinked once. Other than that, she showed no sign of surprise. The Hag had hired her people several times over the years to provide various and usually highly secretive services. Never, though, had the Hag asked her to kill.

"It will cost a lot," she said. "Assassins are few and expensive in Grabentod. I assume you want the best."

The serpent hissed, eyes glowing, and drew back its head as if to strike. A negotiating plot, of course, Haltengabben thought.

She didn't have time for such games today. Stepping forward, she slid a long curved blade from inside her sleeve, then pricked the serpent under its chin. A single drop of oily black blood appeared.

The serpent hissed, but faintly this time, and slowly those glowing red eyes turned dark again.

"No tricks, Hag," she said. Haltengabben hid her distaste behind a smile. "If you don't like the price, you can find someone else. We have no need of your patronage here."

"Sssssso," it hissed. "A pound of gold for his death, Haltengabben. No more."

"Agreed." She returned the blade to its armsheath, crossed to her desk, and sat.

The serpent had already begun to fade. The Hag's sendings were getting stronger, she thought uneasily. Whatever powers the abomination controlled, she certainly used them to good effect.

Haltengabben chewed her lip thoughtfully. This stranger . . . she'd heard something of him already from her spies on the docks. What had they said? A man in his early thirties, wearing green robes, with a long black beard . . . a man who made friends quickly with Bowspear. An ally in his grab for the throne? Perhaps . . . or perhaps something else. Might he somehow pose a threat to the Hag?

She considered that possibility for a moment. The Hag controlled a barren, unpopulated area of the Drachenaur Mountains to the east. That land offered little of importance, and it had no great natural resources to speak of. Only the Hag and her minions . . . and the Hag's reputed treasure.

In the decades since the Hag had assumed her powers, quite a few adventurers had set out to rid Cerilia of her. Few of them had come back. The Hag, rumor said, had accumulated vast stores of weapons, armor, and gold taken from these foolhardy adventurers.

Now, what would Bowspear need to help him seize Grabentod for his own? Nothing but weapons, armor, and gold, she thought smugly. How simply everything fell into place. This stranger must be a warrior of great prowess . . . or a wizard.

Picking up the small golden dagger she used as a letter opener, Haltengabben considered her options. She could have the stranger killed now, possibly angering Bowspear and pleasing the Hag, or she could wait a little longer and see what developed. If the man in green killed the Hag, that treasure would make a tidy prize. She could kill the stranger afterward, fulfilling the word (if not the intent) of her contract with the Hag, and collect his share, too.

Her decision made, she slammed the dagger point first into the much-nicked desktop. It stood there, quivering faintly, and Haltengabben began to smile. Yes, she'd figured it out now.

ANUIRE

five

With a deep feeling of satisfaction, Candabraxis surveyed his study. Harlmut had given him the entire fourth floor of the eastern tower. It consisted of four large rooms, each shaped like a wedge of pie with a bite taken out of the pointy end. (The stairs wound upward in a spire occupying the center column of the tower.)

Four whole rooms, and all for him. He grinned, deliriously happy. Truly, they knew how to treat a wizard in Grabentod.

The room that caught the morning sun would be

his workroom, he thought, wandering in to look around. It was bare at the moment, but when he closed his eyes he could imagine a huge worktable spread with scrolls, jars of rare herbs, and his magic books. A few tapestries on the walls . . . yes, it would do nicely. He went into the north room and quickly decided to make it a study, a warm cozy place where he could entertain visiting wizards and other guests. The south room . . . his library, perhaps? He paused in the doorway, then nodded. Yes, he would find an apprentice or two and teach in here. They could sleep on the floor, on pallets. The west room, catching the evening sun, would be his bedchamber. It already had a canopied featherbed and wardrobe, and that's where Bowspear's men had left his bags.

One of the castle's countless servants had already unpacked his clothing and put it away. They had left his books, papers, scrolls, and magical paraphernalia alone.

He threw himself on the bed, laughing, and closed his eyes. Feathers! And so soft, he seemed to be floating on air. With a contented sigh, he thought back to the thin hard pallets his old master had insisted upon. "They build character," Master Razlev had said knowingly. Privately, the other apprentices and journeymen had whispered about cheapness.

Candabraxis sat up and looked around the bedroom. Yes, it would do quite nicely for the moment, he thought. First things first, though. He sat up and crossed to his crate of books. He needed to look up a few names in his copy of *Morweit's Peerage*. If he could find some way to help with King Graben's return, he knew his position here would be secure forever.

He drew out the thick, heavy volume and lugged it to the bed. One of his first tasks as an apprentice had been to meticulously copy Razlev's volume of *Morweit's Peerage*. At first it had been an exercise in penmanship—Candabraxis noted, as he leafed through it, how cramped and sloppy the first hundred pages looked—but gradually it had become a work of love. He had finally finished copying all eight hundred and sixty-three pages (plus two slender supplemental volumes) a year and a half after he'd begun, and at that point his script had been every bit as graceful and meticulous as Razlev's own. Plus he'd neatly added family crests in the narrow margins whenever he had been able to locate them.

He leafed forward to Müden and began skimming the family lines, memorizing names. Wizards had to remember vast amounts of information, and memory training had been a large part of Razlev's early teachings.

"Alborgac . . . Achpelkar . . . Avacht," he began, reading aloud. There wouldn't be more than two or three hundred names. And he had only to match one of them in Grabentod or one of the neighboring realms.

* * * * *

An hour later Candabraxis, closed the second supplement to the *Peerage*. The results had been singularly disappointing, he thought. Only one name had turned up with any links to the ruling merchant families in Müden. The Erbrechts, perhaps the most powerful and wealthy (and, therefore, the most influential) of Müden's merchant families, had married a fifth-born daughter into Drachenward's ruling family, forty years earlier. That daughter, Helga Erbrecht, had married Oluvar Hawk, a prince of the realm. Their firstborn son (who would, technically, be seventeenth in line to the Erbrecht family fortune) would be an ideal choice to ransom back for King Graben. Unfortunately, the *Peerage* had no information on this son . . . not even a name. Still, perhaps someone here would know of him.

At the very least, it gave him something to tell Harlmut at the feast tonight. Candabraxis puffed out his chest a little. A feast in *his* honor. If only Razlev and his friends could have seen him now.

He opened one of the windows and leaned out, breathing the crisp cold air. The sun had begun its long slow slide to the west, and as he gazed out over the streets and houses of Grabentod, again that strange sense of familiarity touched him. Staring down, watching the sparkle of sunlight on water, he felt his mood shift. Somberly, he pondered again what strange forces had drawn him here.

* * * * *

By the time Parniel Bowspear reached the castle gates, darkness had fallen. He had attended enough of Harlmut's interminable "feasts" to expect the worst: adequate food and dull court gossip. Of course, Harlmut sat at the head of the table in King Graben's place, stiff and wooden as always. He only made matters worse. Rather than leading the conversations the way King Graben did, he merely nodded at the talk around him, trying not to offend anyone.

Bowspear arrived late, planning to finish the main course and make his escape at the most opportune time. After his initial shock had worn off, he regretted fleeing the Temple of Ela. Tonight he would return for his meeting with Haltengabben. He still needed her support.

As he crossed the courtyard and headed for the banquet hall, though, sounds of music and laughter from ahead caught him by surprise. The three court musicians were playing a sprightly tune on horns, cymbals, and lute. He hadn't heard such gaiety since before King Graben had been captured. Suddenly everyone began to applaud.

Frowning, Bowspear quickened his step. The guard swung the door open for him, and he strode into the huge banquet hall. Overhead, all three chandeliers had been lit, and hundreds of tallow candles provided a warm yellow glow.

Bowspear shrugged off his heavy gray cloak and handed it to one of the servants. The long banquet table, although loaded with food, was lined with empty chairs. The guests had left their places to watch . . . *dancing?*

He wandered forward, staring in disbelief as Candabraxis and Lady Delma, the king's wife, swept around the room one last time, then ended in a graceful pirouette. The entire court began to applaud enthusiastically. After a second's hesitation, he joined in. It wouldn't be fitting for him to snub Lady Delma. Although he found her as shallow as a rain puddle, her influence stretched almost as far as his own.

Candabraxis bowed to Lady Delma, then offered her his arm. She accepted, giggling a little, and he escorted her back to the banquet table. Everyone else followed, talking excitedly. Bowspear hid his frown of displeasure. It seemed Candabraxis had made quite an impression on the whole court already. And Harlmut, beaming at everyone and everything around him, looked almost regal himself for the first time. He seemed to have regained much of the confidence he had lost in recent months.

It had to be Candabraxis, Bowspear thought with growing displeasure. Somehow, the two of them had forged an alliance. Nevertheless, he forced a broad smile. Alliance or not, it wouldn't save Harlmut, he vowed.

"I'm sorry I'm late for your feast," he said to Candabraxis. "I lost track of the hour, cataloging our cargo from the last voyage."

"Oh, surely you have people who can do that sort of thing," Lady Delma said dismissively.

"Of course, but I want it done right." He bowed to her. "I must say, you're looking even more radiant than usual, Lady Delma."

She blushed a little. "Thank you, Parniel."

Bowspear turned to his regular seat at Harlmut's right hand—and found the wizard already in it. Still, that was to be expected: Candabraxis was the guest of honor. He took the seat next to the wizard, displacing fat old Lord Korgaard, and the whole side of the table shifted accordingly. They knew better than to challenge him.

Servants began pouring more goblets of wine and bringing out platters of hot roasted chicken, a whole pig with an apple in its mouth, and small loaves of crusty bread. Bowspear took a long drink of his wine, then found the wizard nodding pleasantly to him.

He nodded back. "How do you find Grabentod?" he asked, trying to be polite.

"Cold."

A laugh went up around the table. Candabraxis grinned.

Cold. Bowspear felt like rolling his eyes.

"What other new dances do you know?" Lady Delma asked, fanning herself. She seated herself in her normal place, at Harlmut's left hand.

"Oh, I'm sure I know three or four more that haven't made it here yet," the wizard said modestly. His face was a little flushed from exertion, but he seemed almost exuberant. "Perhaps, at your next formal ball . . ."

"Of course," she said determinedly. "We *must* have a formal ball. Elastide is in ten days. We shall hold it then. With your permission, *of course*," she said, looking to Harlmut.

He made a small gesture. "Whenever Lady

Delma desires."

She gave a squeal of delight, turned to Lady Jasmar, two seats to her left, and began discussing decorations. *As a puddle,* Bowspear thought. Now, thanks to Candabraxis, he'd have *another* awful social function to attend. He began to wish he'd quietly dropped the wizard overboard on the way back to Grabentod.

"Tell me," Harlmut said loudly to the wizard, leaning forward, "what has your research turned up?"

Bowspear felt a jab of apprehension. Research—that sounded like trouble. Watching Candabraxis from the corner of his eye, he helped himself to a loaf of bread.

"Well," Candabraxis said, between bites of a chicken leg, "according to *Morweit's Peerage,* the nearest relatives of Müden's ruling Erbrecht family are in Drachenward. Forty years ago, Barke Erbrecht married one of his daughters to a prince of Drachenward, Oluvar Hawk. Their firstborn son would be, technically, seventeenth in line for the Erbrecht family's fortune."

"Hawk . . . I know that name," Bowspear murmured. Where had he heard it before?

Candabraxis turned to him. "Oh? And do you know if he has a son?"

He grinned inwardly, as it all came back to him. "Yes, he does," he said. He could reveal it since it could do Harlmut no good. "His name is Orin Hawk, I believe."

"Orin Hawk—" Harlmut said. Then his expression

turned to one of dismay. "Oh."

Candabraxis looked from Bowspear to Harlmut and back again. "Is there some problem? Is he dead?"

"Tell him," Bowspear said.

"Orin Hawk," Harlmut said, "is in thrall to the Hag. He led a squad of men from Drachenward on a mission to kill her or drive her from her lair some years ago. Rather than kill him, she charmed him and his men. Now they serve her utterly, guarding her border with Drachenward."

Candabraxis laughed. "Excellent!" he cried. "This is perfect!"

"How so?" Bowspear demanded cautiously.

"What better way to win Müden's favor? If you capture Hawk and pull him back from the Hag's evil, then return him, fully restored, to Drachenward, it might well persuade the king of Drachenward to intercede on your behalf."

"Impossible!" Bowspear said. "It would be a foolhardy mission. We all know what the Hag does to those who venture into her lands. She charms them. She toys with them. Then she kills them. The few who return to civilized lands have addled minds, for they have seen visions too terrible for mortals to bear."

"Is this true?" Candabraxis asked, looking to Harlmut.

Unhappily, the regent nodded. "I fear he is beyond our reach. Who of us would dare try to retrieve him from the Hag?"

"I would!" cried a voice farther down the table.

"And who will join me?"

"I will!" answered a second, then a third, then a half dozen more men.

Shocked, Bowspear glanced to his left. Captain Evann stood there, his bearded face drawn with determination. Slowly Evann's piercing gray eyes turned to Bowspear.

"I fear the Hag," he said, "but I want our king back more. If we must save Orin Hawk from her, so be it. With a wizard's help, surely we must succeed. The alternative is unacceptable."

Bowspear swallowed. That last remark seemed to have been directed at him. Evann had long been a rival . . . and now it seemed Evann hoped to win especial favor by taking on the Hag and her creatures.

"I will prepare protective charms for you," Candabraxis said firmly. "Every protection I can offer will be yours."

"This is madness," Bowspear scoffed. He felt a rising uneasiness. With a wizard's help, he realized their mad plan might have a slight chance of success. Surely the Hag would never expect an attack. And if they actually succeeded in saving Hawk from her . . .

"Thank you," Harlmut was saying. He stood and raised his cup. "A toast to Captain Evann!" he cried. "May he save Orin Hawk . . . and our king!"

Or die trying, Bowspear mentally added. He forced a smile and raised his cup.

"To Captain Evann," he said. "May he get all that he truly deserves."

Eh, lad? Orin Hawk? Aye, I heard of that one—one of the Hag's minions.

As any fool knows, the Hag uses her powers to entrap anybody who ventures into her domain. Orin Hawk should have known it—he was a nobleman from Drachenward, after all—but somehow he got the notion in his head to drive her from her lands. He gathered forty men and marched them straight into the heart of her domain.

That was the last time Drachenward heard from Hawk. Aye, ye've guessed right. The Hag charmed them all and holds 'em in her power to this day.

Like my pappy always said, best steer clear of magic . . . mark that lesson well, lad.

six

Parniel Bowspear returned to the Temple of Ela just after midnight. When he entered the front doors, he found an underpriest standing there, waiting for him. The man wore long black robes, with a black skullcap on his shaved head, and his features were gaunt and pinched, almost emaciated. His pale blue eyes missed nothing, though, as he studied Bowspear's face.

"Is she here?" he asked.

"This way," the underpriest said, turning toward the altar room. "Haltengabben is expecting you."

Bowspear hesitated a moment before ducking through the doorway after him, but when he did, he found no trace of the bizarre ceremony he had witnessed earlier. The large brass braziers still smoked, but now they let off the scents of sweetly aromatic herbs, and the dancers, musicians, and giant serpent had vanished entirely.

The priest led him past the altar and through a maze of tiny corridors to Haltengabben's overcrowded office. When he entered, she looked up from a manuscript, then quickly rolled it up and put it away.

"About this morning—" he began.

"It's not important," she said. "Sit."

Meekly, he slid into one of the chairs before her desk. Somehow she managed to make him feel small whenever he was in her presence. He intensely disliked that feeling. But I need her, he told himself, far more than she needs me.

"You brought a wizard to Grabentod," she stated flatly.

Of course her spies would have informed her about the wizard. Nothing happened in Grabentod that she didn't know about. Doubtless she knew more about the cargo he'd captured last night than he did.

"Yes," he said slowly. "He was on his way to Müden when I captured his ship—"

"He will lead only to trouble," she said, interrupting. "But there is a chance for great profit."

"Then you know about the expedition?" he asked. He wondered at her spy network. The expedition had been agreed upon only a few hours ago, and he had been the first to leave the feast.

"Of course . . . and I want you to represent my interests in it as well."

He regarded her suspiciously. "How?" And what exactly did she mean by her interests?

Haltengabben stood and began to pace. "The wizard will doubtless provide charms that may prove useful against the Hag's lesser creatures."

"He did promise something of the sort," Bowspear murmured.

"*I* can provide you with something better . . . an amulet that will render you invisible to her creatures." She lifted an intricately carved wooden box from a shelf and drew out a long silver chain. A pendant set with what looked like a large ruby eye dangled from it. "Behold, the Eye of Vadakkar."

Bowspear stood. *Invisibility.* With that amulet, he realized, he could follow Evann into the Hag's Domain. With that amulet, he could make certain Evann's mission failed.

"How does it work?"

"The wearer and anyone within twenty feet of the Eye is protected from scrying. The Hag will never know you're in her territory."

"And what is your price?"

"Half."

He paled a little. "Half of what?" he asked.

She smiled. "*Everything.*"

Bowspear bit his lip. He could take Grabentod's crown without her, but only if Evann failed. If the king returned . . . if the king found out all that Bowspear had been doing in his absence . . .

But half of Grabentod as the price!

Then he smiled. The people would never accept her as their queen. She would have to stay comfortably behind the scenes, much as she did now. Half . . . perhaps it wouldn't be nearly as much as it sounded like now.

"How does it work?" he asked.

* * * * *

Dawn brought slate-gray skies and a cold, steady wind from the north. As Captain Terrill Evann mustered his squad of ten men in the castle's courtyard, he felt two of his ribs ache with the promise of snow.

He'd broken those ribs in his first mission as a Grabentod Raider eighteen years before, when one of Müden's royal marines had leapt inside his guard and punched him in the chest with the pommel of his sword. He'd been lucky to live through that battle. He wouldn't have if King Graben hadn't cut the marine down with one powerful blow from his sword. If he could repay that debt now, he would.

Scowling, he stared up at the sky as the first few snowflakes drifted lazily toward the ground. Not the most auspicious omen, he thought. Still, this early in the season, the mountain passes would be clear. He and his men were used to the snow. As long as they did not tarry, they should get back safely.

Assuming they found Orin Hawk.

Assuming the wizard's charms worked.

Assuming the Hag didn't kill them.

He stopped in front of Uwe Taggart, the youngest of his volunteers at seventeen. He'd had half a mind to refuse the lad's request to join . . . but Uwe'd already fought, and fought well, in two sea battles. Uwe's young, deep-blue eyes stared expressionlessly back at Evann. He'd been letting the soft downy yellow hair on his cheeks grow, and over the last month, it had lengthened into a sketchy beard. A man now, indeed, Evann realized; he couldn't very well refuse him.

"Open your pack," he said gruffly.

"Yes, sir." Uwe squatted, unlaced the flaps on his backpack, and began laying out the contents on the flagstones. Bedroll, candles, rope, dried jerked meat, canteen—all the supplies he'd been ordered to bring. Evann nodded: he'd expected no less.

"It'll do," he said. "Shut it."

Nodding as Uwe began reassembling his pack, Evann moved to the next man, Ivar Reddman, and did likewise. He knew they'd all have their full marching kits ready, though; this was an exercise to kill time.

With a glance at the east tower, he wondered how long the wizard planned to take. Candabraxis had left the feast, even though technically it was in his honor, to begin preparations to leave.

* * * * *

Parniel Bowspear dangled the Eye of Vadakkar

before a candle, watching the play of red light and shadow as different facets of the ruby caught the flickering glow. Deep inside the stone, he thought he saw movement, a shape that flitted first one way, and then another.

Abruptly he blinked, pulled the chain over his head, and tucked the stone inside his tunic. Dawn had nearly come; he still had a lot to do before then.

Pulling a set of chain mail from a trunk by his bed, he began hooking it on. Despite Haltengabben's promise of invisibility to the Hag's scrying, he planned on taking no chances. That meant wearing the armor he'd taken from a prince of Massenmarch last year, wielding his good long sword, and bringing twelve of his best men.

They would find Hawk first, he vowed, and kill him. Or, if the opportunity presented itself, they would ambush Evann and his men. He had several old scores to settle with Captain Evann . . . he hadn't forgotten the first year of his own captaincy, when Evann had time and again reminded King Graben of Bowspear's youth and inexperience. As a result, Evann had taken more than his fair share of prize ships, leaving lesser targets for Bowspear.

Finished with his armor, he rose, opened the door, and glanced up and down the street. Dawn had just begun to touch the east with fingers of gray. His breath misted before him. It would snow today, he thought: so much the better. It would make tracking Evann easier.

He strode out to round up his men.

* * * * *

The last of the magic spells finally cast, Candabraxis sank back in the chair next to his worktable. He had carefully unpacked the ingredients he used in his more complex conjurations, and they covered the table now, a jumbled mass of jars, vials, boxes, packets, and other containers.

He pressed his eyes shut and gave a low groan. He ached from mind to body. There was simply no other way to put it. Magic always took a lot out of a wizard, but spell after spell, cast in rapid succession throughout the night, left him with a deep psychic hurt that his body now mirrored.

Forcing himself back to his feet, he took a deep swallow from the glass of water on the table, then looked appreciatively at the eleven talismans he had created. To the untrained eye, each one looked like a carved obsidian pin in the shape of a wolf. Unlike mere glass, however, each talisman carried deep within a magical charge potent enough to deflect a variety of spells. Not all spells, of course—no mere talisman could do that—but the magic he had imbued in each pin would certainly protect its wearer against some of the most common and potentially lethal castings, such as unnatural fears and petrifications.

He donned a heavy woolen cloak, gathered up the talismans, and began the long descent to ground level. Next time someone offered him a suite of rooms in a tower, he vowed, he'd ask for a lower floor.

When at last, panting a bit, he opened the tower door and stepped into the courtyard, he found a light snow just beginning to fall. Captain Evann and his squad of men stood across from him, going through a weapons check of some kind.

Captain Evann spotted him and jogged to his side. "Are they—?" he called.

"Done. Yes." Candabraxis held out the small cloth sack he'd placed the talismans in. "Here."

Evann drew one out and stared at it. "How do they work?" he asked.

"Pin it to your clothing—it doesn't matter where. That's all you need to do."

He scowled at it. "It doesn't seem like much. . . ."

"It will protect you against all minor charms and spells . . . not against the Hag herself, certainly, but it should work against any magics used by her minions."

He nodded. "It will be enough," he said.

Evann returned to his men and began handing them out. The men, one by one, pinned the talismans to their cloaks.

The doors to the audience hall opened, and Harlmut strode out. Like Candabraxis, he wore a heavy woolen cloak with the hood pulled up. He quickly joined Captain Evann and talked in quiet tones with him. Evann nodded several times, called orders to his men, and marched them single file out through the huge castle gates. Outside, they turned toward the Drachenaur Mountains. Candabraxis watched until the last one had vanished from sight behind the walls.

Harlmut joined him.

"What are their chances of finding Hawk?" Candabraxis asked. By the light of day, it seemed a mad, almost impossible plan.

"They will succeed," Harlmut said firmly. "They have to."

* * * * *

The door to Haltengabben's office burst open, and a boy of perhaps ten or eleven rushed up to the desk. Young Jerroch. Haltengabben had assigned him to watch the castle. Something must have happened there, she realized, but that was no excuse for his behavior, not here in the Temple of Ela.

"Always knock, Jerroch," she said sternly.

"But, Haltengabben—" he gasped.

"Do it again."

Slowly, head down, he turned and went back out into the hall, pulling the door closed after him. A heartbeat later, he gave a timid rap.

"Come in!" Haltengabben called.

He opened the door, stepped in, and pulled it closed after him. Taking his place solemnly before her desk, head bowed, he waited for her to speak first. She nodded imperceptibly: much better. She kept an iron discipline inside the temple.

"Make your report," she said.

"The soldiers left, Haltengabben."

"How many?"

"Ten, Haltengabben."

"And the wizard?"

"He stayed at the castle."

Haltengabben leaned back in her seat, pursing her lips slightly. So . . . Candabraxis hadn't gone along on the mission. She'd expected him to try to kill the Hag himself. Perhaps he didn't want the strength of her bloodline. But what manner of magical weapons must he have given to the soldiers to safely battle her? And why risk passing the Hag's bloodline along to one of them? It didn't make sense. She had missed something somewhere, she decided.

"Thank you," she said to the boy. She opened a small pouch on the desk, drew out a copper eagle, and tossed the coin to him. He tucked it into his belt in one swift movement. "That will be all," she said.

"Yes, Haltengabben." Bobbing his head once, he turned and quietly left her office, shutting the door carefully and almost silently behind him.

Candabraxis posed a threat, she decided. She couldn't have him lingering in Alber. No telling what mischief he might discover.

After a second's thought, she drew a small, square piece of parchment from a stack, dipped her quill pen in ink, and began to write a brief letter explaining the situation.

Her sister Temple of Ela in Grevesmühl had an assassin staying with them at the moment. The price would be steep, but she knew she could buy his services to kill the wizard and still make a tidy profit, thanks to the Hag. After all, a pound of gold went a long way in Grabentod.

ANUIRE

seven

Captain Evann couldn't help noticing the high
spirits of his men as they marched in two columns
out of Alber. He had seldom seen a more enthusi-
astic band of adventurers. And why not? They
were off to save the king, and with a wizard's
magic to protect them, they had no doubts as to
their ultimate success.

He arched his back a little as he led them up the
road. This early, no one had turned out to see them
off, and just as well. The fewer people who saw
them leave, the less talk there would be.

Cobbles rapidly gave way to deeply rutted wagon tracks as they left the city. With the wind at their backs, the snow little more than flurries, and gently rolling farmlands before them, he knew they would make good time today.

He squinted at the horizon. Twenty miles ahead, the immense Drachenaur Mountains began. He planned to march out to the foothills, turn right, and skirt them until they came to the Hag's Domain. It would take four or five days of steady marching.

For now, the company had nothing to worry about. Today would be the easiest stage of the trip, as they crossed the most civilized part of Grabentod. Idly, Evann stared at the fields surrounding them. In the spring, the land would be green with wheat and oats and hay, but for now he saw only a few animals loose to graze on winter-brown grass and thistles: cattle, a handful of mules and horses, some goats.

He grinned as, behind him, he heard Harrach begin a boisterous marching song. "The Ballad of Gretta Magree" was a catchy tune, and one he hadn't heard since King Graben's brief campaign against the neighboring barony of Wolfgaard, some ten years before. He found himself matching his stride to the tempo. The three battles against the baron had been indecisive, and when winter came, both sides had withdrawn from their mutual border. Hostilities had never resumed, though the peace remained uneasy.

The rest of Evann's men joined in on the bawdy

chorus the second time Harrach sang it, even Uwe Taggart, whose clear young voice rang like a bell in the stillness.

Late in the morning, the snow let up completely, leaving a faint dusting on the ground. Overhead, the clouds parted, and briefly the company glimpsed a wan sun.

At noon Evann called a break, and after a quick lunch of trail rations washed down by water from a stream, they continued as before. They had a lot of ground to travel today, he knew, if they were going to reach the foothills below Mount Krakenwald, the closest of the Drachenaur Mountains, before darkness overtook them.

The day wore on, the road became rougher, and the farms fewer and farther between. Harrach moved from lusty ballads to military marching songs until his voice gave out, and then the men chatted as they walked. Evann listened with half an ear, but mostly kept his attention on the road ahead.

The mountains grew steadily closer. Although he'd been this far only twice before—both times as King Graben's guest on hunting expeditions—Evann remembered it well enough. He'd never thought he'd enjoy himself so far from the sea, but the hunting, feasting, and general merrymaking had been quite an experience. At the end of the first hunt, King Graben had made him captain of one of his roundboats. Truly, it had been a week to remember. He smiled as he thought back on it all.

As afternoon edged into evening, the sun beginning to stretch the men's shadows long before them, they reached the dense pine forest that marked the beginning of wilderness. The roar of a cougar came from somewhere close by, and several deer bolted for safety among the trees.

Here the road ended entirely. Several small trails, suitable for little more than small game, wound up into the pines. Evann paused, inhaling the fresh, clean-scented air and trying to get his bearings. Which trail had they taken last time to get to the king's hunting lodge?

The one on the left, he thought. He peered in that direction. Just visible over the trees he spotted what looked like wooden shingles . . . a roof? It had to be.

"This way," Evann announced, starting forward. "We'll spend the night at the king's hunting lodge. It's just ahead."

A cheer came from his men. No roughing it out in the cold tonight, he thought with a quick grin.

The trail twisted several times, climbing a rocky hill dotted with trees. When at last a broad clearing opened before him, he found the lodge almost exactly as he had remembered it: a huge log building, perhaps eighty feet long and forty feet deep, with its back up against a stone cliff. It had four large chimneys, two at each end, and ten broad windows across the front. All the windows had been securely shuttered. Nobody had been here in the years since King Graben's capture, and it showed. Dirt, pine needles, and dead branches lay everywhere, and a few shingles had blown off the roof, exposing sun-bleached thatch. Still, it would more than do for their purposes.

He walked up to the front door as though he owned the lodge, tried the knob, and found it locked. For a second he frowned, wishing he'd thought to ask Harlmut for the key, but then he set his shoulder to the door and heaved. The latch gave way with a squeal of twisting metal, and he stumbled inside.

"Open the shutters," he said, stepping inside and shrugging off his pack. The main room was almost completely dark. The air inside had a dank, musty, deserted smell. He blinked quickly, trying to identify the dark shapes of furniture in the dimness, then moved forward.

Light flooded in as first one, then another, then another of the windows came open. Evann dumped his pack on the long table in the center of the room, stirring up puffs of dust. Stuffed animal heads—deer, elk, cougars, a couple of bears—covered the walls. Plenty of comfortable chairs circled the stone fireplace, and padded leather couches stood up against the walls. Doors led to private bedchambers, the kitchens, and the servants' quarters.

His men trooped after him. He heard a few exclamations of surprise and pleasure.

"Harrach, Wolfgar, set a fire," he said. "Turach, see if you can find oil and lamps."

They would spend the night in this room, he decided. Once they had a fire going and the place warmed up, it would be as cozy as home. There was nothing like a hunting lodge for comfort.

Evann clapped his hands together to warm them and nodded in satisfaction. Yes, this would do quite nicely, he thought. Now, to see if any wine remained in the cellars . . .

As he turned for the kitchens, a loud grating noise came from one of the back rooms. He paused for a heartbeat.

"What was that?" he demanded, turning and counting heads quickly. All his men were here.

They glanced at one another uneasily, then back at him. He swallowed. They weren't alone.

Holding up one hand for silence, he drew his sword, then crept cautiously toward the doors at the back of the room. Now that he listened, he heard a faint scratching sound coming from one. It sounded like iron rubbing on stone. The hairs on the back of his neck began to bristle. This room had belonged to King Graben, he recalled.

Hardly breathing, Evann pressed his ear to the door, straining to hear. After a second, the *scritch-scritch* sound came again, followed by a scuttling noise.

Probably just animals, he thought. Maybe a family of raccoons had gotten inside. Still, best to be careful. . . .

Silently, he held up four fingers, pointed to the door, then pantomimed walking around the lodge. Harrach, Taggart, Reddman, and Lothar drew their swords and padded silently out the door. They would cover that room's windows from outside. The rest of his men eased out their own swords as well.

Evann counted to twenty, waiting for Harrach and the others to get into position, then stepped forward and flung the door open.

He found himself facing a huge black bear. It stood by the king's bed, facing him, perhaps fifteen feet away.

Letting out a roar, it reared up. Its head just missed the ceiling twelve feet above. Then, growling deep in its throat, it dropped to four feet and charged straight at him.

Evann slammed the door in its face. He'd hunted a bear the last time he'd come out to the lodge with King Graben, but the one they'd found had been half the size of this one. He'd never seen anything so huge on land before. He knew it could tear a man in half without much effort. Hopefully the door would stop it.

Instead of giving up, though, the bear rammed into the closed door with enough force to crack its wooden frame. Then, using its front paws, it began to punch its way through. The door shuddered under its weight, then made a splintering sound.

"Back!" Evann shouted, and his men gave way. "Get your crossbows!" he ordered. "That's our best bet!"

They ran for their packs. He held his ground, long sword ready. Suddenly, the bear punched a hole through the middle of the door with one huge, clawed paw. Reaching out, it tried to grab him.

It was the opportunity he'd been waiting for. Leaping forward, Evann swung the long sword with all his strength, whipping it down in a savage blow and putting all his weight behind it.

The blade bit deep into the creature's forepaw, but didn't sever it, as he'd hoped. Spraying blood, the bear jerked its wounded limb back into the king's chamber. A second later a large eye lowered to the opening and peered out. The bear let loose an angry, strangled scream as it focused on him. It knew he'd been the one to hurt it, Evann realized.

It battered the door again with all its weight. The latch made a cracking sound.

Evann glanced back at his men. Three of them had their crossbows out and were sitting on the floor, cranking back the drawstrings as fast as they could. They weren't going to be ready before the bear broke through, he realized with dismay.

With a crashing sound, the door flew open. The bear paused for a second in the doorway.

Evann held his ground, sword at the ready. His men began to fire, two scattered shots, then a third. The bolts lodged deep in the huge beast's side with dull *thucks*, but seemed to have little effect. If anything, they made it only madder.

Rearing back, blood gushing down its coat, it roared with raw fury. Long strings of blood-flecked saliva dangled from its jaws. Then, as though stung by mosquitoes rather than crossbow bolts, it charged straight at him.

Heart pounding, he raised his long sword, the

point out before him. His hand wavered, but he forced it steady. There could be no flinching now. It was just the two of them, man against beast. He wouldn't go down easily.

The bear impaled itself. He felt the blade slide into its chest like a knife into butter, and then it was on him, bowling him over. He smelled the stink of its breath and felt the wet splash of its drool on his face as it wrapped mammoth paws around his back in a crushing embrace. A foul stench filled his lungs. He couldn't draw in any air. His face crammed against dense black fur.

He tried to shove it back, but it continued to press down on him, throwing him off his feet. He fell backward.

That was the last he knew.

* * * * *

Throughout the day, Bowspear and his men had cautiously but easily trailed Captain Evann and his men. This close to Alber, Bowspear thought, Evann doubtless felt he had nothing to worry about. After all, the Hag's reach barely extended to her own realm's borders, and they would have nothing to worry about from her for several days.

Evann's course took them due east. It didn't take Bowspear long to realize they intended to spend the night at the king's hunting lodge. He nodded; he would have done the same thing himself. Tomorrow, Evann would turn southeast, following the line of mountains to the Drachenlok, the rough river that spilled down from the mountains and into Wolfgaard Bay. From there it would be only a few miles to the mountains separating Grabentod from the Hag's Domain.

Confident he knew Evann's plans, Bowspear turned south at the next crossroads. His uncle had a farm seven or eight miles from here. They could spend the night in his barn, then set out early the next morning. With any luck, and some long, forced marches, they would reach Drachenlok ahead of Captain Evann.

He smiled grimly. And then the fun would begin.

ANUIRE

eight

After seeing Captain Evann off, Candabraxis spent the rest of the morning and most of the afternoon in his rooms asleep. When he finally roused himself, he felt drained, as emotionally and physically exhausted as he'd ever been in his life. Working so much magic at once had taken more out of him than he'd expected. You're getting old, he thought with a chuckle. His old master kept apprentices and journeymen around to help with such castings, and Candabraxis began to appreciate why.

Half aware, drowsing in the land between sleep and wakefulness, he lay in bed and stared up through slitted eyes. Slowly, the plastered ceiling and huge rough-hewn support beams began to spin overhead, then faded to blackness.

Magic. He felt his pulse start to race. Someone had begun to cast a spell that involved him. But who would do that? And why?

Carefully, he kept his body immobile. Let whoever it was think he still slept. His old master had been more than a little paranoid, and he'd taught his students many ways to defend themselves from unwanted scrying. Later tonight he would prepare a talisman to protect himself from magically prying eyes. Now, though, he could do little but bide his time and wait for the perfect moment to strike back.

Something moved in the darkness over him. He saw gigantic dark eyes emerge from the gloom . . . a hideous face covered in boils and open sores . . . long, scraggly white hair. . . .

It had to be the Hag. Somehow he had attracted her attention. He swallowed. The abomination's scrying would be hard to throw off, since she drew her strength from the land and her bloodline, but he had to try. Perhaps, if she wasn't expecting it—

In one sudden movement, he leapt from the bed, chanting now, calling on the primordial forces of Cerilia, drawing upon the land itself as the source of his magical strength. He felt power coursing like a living thing through the land around him, rushing up into his body. He became a channel for it, directing it toward the darkness over him.

Light and energy burst from his hands, streaming upward in a brilliant arc. He pressed his eyes closed, and still the blinding light pounded into his skull. He heard himself start to scream, but whether it was from pain or ecstasy, he didn't know.

Abruptly, he was alone. Flames covered the ceiling of his room, and the heavy beams burned with hot embers.

With a quick gesture, he doused the fire. Smoke curled in the air before him, then slowly dissipated.

Drawing a shuddering breath, he sank down on the bed. It had been a simple child's trick, directing the power of the land up into the lens of the scrying spell the Hag had used. In effect, he had flashed a bright light into her eyes. It wouldn't have hurt her, but might have blinded her for a few seconds. That had been enough to disrupt her spell.

He drew himself upright. No telling how much time he had. Better start work on that protective spell. He'd shield his rooms first, then build a talisman to protect himself when he went out.

He headed for his workshop.

* * * * *

Captain Evann came awake with a jolt of pain.

His men were dragging the dead carcass of the bear off of him, and one claw snagged his cheek, cutting a deep scratch. Shuddering a little, Evann tried to sit up. Uwe Taggart ran to help him. The lad had a canteen out, and Evann sipped gratefully.

"What happened?" he asked.

"It grabbed you and knocked you down," Taggart said, his eyes big, "and we thought you were dead. We all went crazy—everyone rushed it, and then there were swords flying and blood everywhere—"

Evann nodded and climbed to his feet a little unsteadily. His legs felt weak, and his ribs and back ached, but he didn't think he'd broken anything. Touching his cheek, he found blood.

"Just another battle scar," he said with a forced grin. "Nothing to worry about."

Taggart nodded, looking a little awed. Leaders had to be inspiring, Evann knew; his men would take tales of this adventure back to Grabentod with them, and he wanted everyone to know not even a bear could kill him. Let Bowspear try to top *that!*

Turning to his men, he watched them drag the carcass outside. The bear had to weigh seven or eight hundred pounds, he realized. He'd been lucky. It could easily have killed him.

He followed them out. Harrach had already thrown a couple of ropes over a strong branch of a nearby pine, and as Evann watched, they hoisted the bear five feet off the ground. Blood poured from its wounds. Harrach opened a few more to properly drain it.

"Ready to carve soon enough," the grizzled warrior proclaimed. "We'll have good eating tonight!"

"Any sign of other bears about?" Evann asked.

Wolfgar shook his head. "Already checked, sir. Ain't no others. This one here broke through the shutters and holed up inside for the winter."

Evann nodded. "Good. Harrach, see to the butchering."

"Aye, sir."

Circling to the right of the lodge, Evann came to a well. He moved the wooden cover and lowered the bucket. It came up full of clear cold water, which he used to wash the blood from his face. The stink of the animal lingered on him. Its blood covered him from head to heel. He'd have to wash his clothes. In this weather, he didn't look forward to it.

Maybe the king or some of the other nobles had left spare clothes behind, he thought. He turned and went back inside. He found Taggart using kitchen rags to clean up the blood on the floor. Stepping around the mess, Evann went to the king's chamber first.

The bear had broken through a side window's shutter. Bits of wood lay scattered across the floor. The featherbed was in hopeless, fouled ruins, and the paneled walls bore long gouges where the beast had sharpened its claws. Other than that the lodge had little damage. Crossing to the untouched wardrobe, Evann pulled open the doors and looked at the racks of hunting clothes inside. King Graben had a bit more belly than he did, but otherwise they had about the same height and build: everything should fit.

He selected brown pants, a pale green shirt, and fresh undergarments. By the time he'd changed and wandered back out into the common room, Taggart had finished cleaning up and the other men had built a roaring fire. They all sat in front of it, warming their hands and passing around a couple of bottles of wine from the king's stores.

"See if you can find hammer and nails to fix the shutters," he said to Reddman. "No sense leaving it open for more animals."

"Aye, sir," he said, rising with a groan and heading for the kitchens.

Realizing that Harrach was missing, Evann went outside to see how the butchering was coming. His old friend had just begun carving up the carcass. Mouth watering at the thought, Evann sat back to wait. Rank had its privileges, and he planned to have the first steak off the fire.

He'd more than earned it.

ANUIRE

nine

Over the next few days, Parniel Bowspear led his men southeast across gently rolling farmlands and through patches of dense forest. Settlements became fewer and farther between, though there were numerous signs that people had once dwelt here—an abandoned logging camp, tracks and trails, a few deserted farmsteads.

The company made good time, and at noon on the third day, they came to the Drachenlok, the wide, rough river spilling down from the Drachenaur Mountains into Wolfgaard Bay.

Bowspear stood on the bank, gazing across the river for a few moments. Though lower than in the summer months, when melting snow sent it flooding over its banks, the channel was still vast and imposing, easily five hundred yards across. And, at this time of year, it would be cold as ice. He didn't look forward to swimming. How would Evann plan on crossing? Probably at a ford. Bowspear thought he'd once heard of one just into the mountains to their left.

"This way," he said, turning and heading upriver. They had to be at least half a day ahead of Evann, and Bowspear didn't want to lose his lead.

Once they were across, there would be two ways into the Hag's Domain. One lay through the pass at Gletscherel Felsen, where another small river fell from the mountains in a dazzling series of waterfalls. The other way lay through the Warde Pass.

Bowspear decided to use Warde Pass. Evann would be interested in speed, and the pass lay half a day's journey closer.

And, it was an excellent place for an ambush. . . .

* * * * *

In Alber, Haltengabben checked the pigeon coop on the roof of the Temple of Ela. While sunning herself in the courtyard behind the temple, she had heard a brief flutter of wings, and sure enough, a familiar-looking gray carrier pigeon had arrived. He now sat perched just outside the coop, cooing softly.

Making a soft crooning sound in reply, Haltengabben reached out, plucked him off the wooden peg, and turned him over to look at his legs.

He wore a message band. She untied it, stuck the pigeon in the coop with the rest of the birds, and quickly headed for her office. This, she knew, was the reply she had been expecting from her sister temple in Grevesmühl.

Once she had locked her door, she sat at her desk and carefully unfolded the tiny piece of parchment. The crablike script held three simple words:

LORAN LEAVES TODAY.

Haltengabben felt a brief burst of elation. They had agreed to the terms she'd offered. Crumpling the parchment, she tossed it into the fire, where it was quickly consumed.

Loran was the assassin's name. He would arrive secretly, by night, coming up the coast in a small black boat. One of her people would meet him, and she would house him in the temple, but the two of them would never meet. That was how these things worked: should anything unfortunate happen, nobody would be able to connect her to him. He would just be a fallen member of the Temple of Ela.

The message would have been sent yesterday, she thought. It would be a two-day trip by boat.

She nodded. That would be soon enough to kill the wizard, she thought.

*   *   *   *   *

Captain Evann paused atop the bank of the Drachenlok, then quickly dropped back, motioning for his men to take cover. They flattened themselves on the ground around him.

"Fishermen," he said. "From Wolfgaard, I think."

In his brief glimpse of the river, he'd seen a small sailing boat moored not far from shore. Two men and a boy had been on board, pulling in nets. They must have set them the night before, and now they were hauling in a day's catch of fish.

Slowly, on his elbows, he eased forward until he could just peer over the top of the riverbank. Sure enough, they hadn't noticed him. They seemed completely caught up in their work. It wouldn't take them long to finish. He'd need a plan quickly.

Harrach crawled up beside him. "We're taking it, aren't we, sir?" he whispered, a broad knowing grin on his face.

"Aye, that's the plan," Evann said. The fishermen's boat would save them quite a bit of walking . . . and it would carry them to Gletscherel Felsen, which would save even more time. The pass through the mountains there was shorter than the one at Warde Pass, where he'd planned to lead his men.

He crawled backward. "Uwe," he said, turning

to the lad, "take off your armor. Your fair hair makes you look enough like a Wolfgaarder to pass for one at this distance. You signal them, and when they come ashore to help, we'll take their boat. . . ."

Taggart grinned and peeled off his leather armor. In his gray tunic, without his sword or helm, he looked even more like a boy . . . slight of stature, surely of no danger to two grown men.

Standing, he jogged down to the edge of the river, cupped his hands to his mouth, and shouted, "*Hulloo!*" as loud as he could, imitating the nasal accent of the Wolfgaarders.

From his hidden vantage point, Evann winced a bit. The kid was overdoing it, he thought. Luckily the wind would hide most of what he said.

One of the men from the skiff "Hullooed" back.

Taggart shouted, "I need help! My boat hit a rock and sank!"

"We'll come ashore and pick you up soon's we're done!" one of the men called. "Wait there!"

Taggart turned, found a rock, and sat patiently. When he tucked his face down in his arms, Evann smiled. He looked cold, beaten, and unhappy . . . exactly like someone who'd just lost a boat.

The fishermen finished pulling in their nets. They seemed to have taken the bait. They raised their sail, turned their boat to the wind, and tacked toward shore.

"Weapons ready," Evann said softly to his men. He eased his long sword from its scabbard. Everyone around him did likewise. "On my command, we charge."

He waited patiently. The boat grew closer. The second he heard its bottom scrape on sand, he leapt to his feet, screamed a war cry, and raced down the bank.

The three people on board looked shocked. Frantically they tried to turn the sail to catch the wind, but by then it was too late. Evann splashed out knee deep in the icy water and threw himself onto the boat's deck.

One man rushed him with a harpoon, but he knocked it aside with his sword and punched the man in the side of the face. He reeled back, dazed, dropping the weapon. Evann put his blade to the man's throat as the rest of his company climbed aboard.

"We don't want to hurt you," he said loudly to the other two, the second man and the boy, who had climbed as far back in the stern as they could. They had terrified expressions on their faces.

"What do you want, our fish?" the first man demanded. He was trying for bravado, but his limp body and pasty white skin told of his true fear. "Take as much as you want. There's plenty."

"I want the boat," Evann growled. "Ashore with you! We'll leave it at Gletscherel Felsen. You can get it there next week."

"But why—"

"None of your concern!" Evann pricked his neck with the sword blade. "Do you agree?"

The man gave a slight nod.

Evann released him. Calling to his companions,

the fisherman sullenly picked up his cap, stuck it on his head, and leapt from the prow of the boat to the riverbank. The other two followed him.

Everyone gave a long cheer, like they'd just won a major battle instead of stolen a boat from barely armed fishermen. Well, let them, Evann thought. It would keep their spirits up.

He headed aft to take the rudder, calling orders. In seconds Harrach and Wolfgar had the sails set, and they glided out smoothly across the river.

Evann steered south, following the river downstream. Rather than cross to the Warde Pass, they would head out to Wolfgaard Bay, across to the Gletscherel River, and then up the river to the falls . . . and the pass they offered.

ANUIRE

ten

In a darkened room, in a lonely town at the foot of the Gletscherel Falls, sat the wizard known as Prattis. He was old and worn and more than a little mad: it showed mostly in his eyes, which held an almost haunted pain.

On the tabletop before him, he had sketched an intricate design full of waving lines and tracings of circles. As he brought his attention to the pattern, it rippled and began to move. Finally, when the lines blurred together, he found himself gazing as though through a clear pool of water at the face of his mistress.

"What news, pretty-pretty?" the Hag asked with a cackle.

"They come," he said. His watchers had seen everything she had predicted. The soldiers had even captured the fishing boat he'd sent out, exactly as the Hag had said.

"When?" she demanded.

"Today, within the hour."

"When you have them, inform me." The Hag smiled. Prattis cackled with glee. She was happy with him. He'd done what she wanted, and now she was happy with him.

"You won't forget our bargain . . . ?" he called.

"Of course not, pretty-pretty. I shall bring you a beautiful bride all for your own."

"I would rather have you, Mistress." He pouted a little. Why didn't she see his devotion? Why didn't she recognize his love for her?

"Pretty-pretty, ours is a doomed romance." She cackled again.

Frowning, Prattis drew a cloth over the pattern. She always said that, he thought. A doomed romance . . . it had a certain appeal.

The Hag's image vanished.

* * * * *

As they sailed up the Gletscherel toward the falls, the wind began to drop. By midafternoon, it hardly filled the sails. Evann frowned; at this rate they'd make better time walking, but he was loath to give up the boat quite yet.

They neared the mountains, which marked the border of the Hag's Domain, and he wondered if her creatures might be watching them from the shore. Candabraxis might have given them protective talismans, but Evann still planned on taking things slowly and cautiously.

Without a breeze, the air grew stifling. Evann found himself staring to their port side, at the shore. It looked singularly inhospitable, since the trees were bare of leaves . . . almost skeletal in winter's embrace, he thought darkly.

"Sir," Uwe called from his perch in the rigging. He was the only one of the crew light enough to climb up there without capsizing the boat. "There's a small town ahead."

"A town?"

Evann turned and squinted. He could see a faint dark smudge far ahead, in the breach where two mountains came together. Ahead, the river continued around one of the mountains to the falls. There, they would find the pass. Something about a town being here disturbed him. He *thought* they were still in Wolfgaard, but who in their right minds would settle so close to the Hag?

If the townsfolk were civilized, it might be a good place to shelter the ship until the wind returned. At the very least, there would be fresh water, fresh food, and most especially a warm place to sleep. He glanced up at the sky. Anyway, it was too late to set out for the pass, he thought. They could do it just as well tomorrow morning.

"We'll put in there for a night!" he announced.

As they drew closer, he saw it was a decently sized town. It sat on a natural inlet of the river. It looked like any of a hundred other fishing villages he had seen over the years, with small docks and perhaps two hundred whitewashed stone houses sprawling up the side of the mountain. Several dozen boats of varying sizes had been tied up or drawn ashore for the night, and bright yellow nets had been spread out to dry in the sun. No fortress or castle brooded over the buildings. Doubtless the place would be run by a local council of elders, or perhaps by some minor noble.

People had already begun to wander down to the docks to point and stare. A few waved.

Evann smiled. It seemed like a pleasant enough place to relax; nothing could bother them here.

They pulled up to an empty dock just as dusk settled over the land. Several boys of seven or eight years came running to take the ropes and moor the boat in place, and after it was secured, Evann hopped to shore.

An old man stepped forward from the knot of townsfolk who'd gathered. He wore baggy white pants and a gray shirt and, atop his head and set at a jaunty angle, an intricately sequined cap. This had to be the town's leader.

"We bid you welcome to Gletscherel Village," the old man said with a slight bow. "I am Ara Mundi, and the hospitality of my house is yours."

Evann bowed in return. "Thank you, sir," he said. "I am Captain Evann. We are passing through on our way to the falls."

"The falls?" Mundi asked. "Why?"

"I am a mapmaker for the Erbrechts of Müden. Doubtless you have heard of them."

Mundi stared blankly back at him. "No. We thought you might be traders, until we saw you were on a fishing boat."

Evann shook his head. "I hired this boat to speed our journey. As I said, I am charting these waters for the Erbrecht family's archives." He indicated the men behind him. "These are my guards."

"You are welcome to stay the night, if you wish. There are several small taverns . . . though our local vintage will doubtless be poor fare for a well-traveled man such as you. There are several shrines to the gods as well, should you wish to make offerings. I trust your stay will be a pleasant one."

"I'm certain it will be."

"There is, however, the matter of the docking tax . . ."

"My assistant Harrach takes care of such matters," Evann said. "See him in the morning, and all will be arranged."

"As you wish." Mundi bowed again. Turning, he motioned to the men and women behind him. "Move along, now! Lanji, Cerji—don't you have homes and wives to attend to? And Kaeli! What about your shop? You'd leave it to your sons to run? I thought not!" All the people turned and started to wander off, looking faintly disappointed.

In a moment, the dock was deserted. Evann looked up and down, but saw no one anywhere. Few lights showed in any of the windows; no voices disturbed the stillness of the air. Not even a dog or a rooster broke the silence. He shivered. The place seemed empty and eerily quiet. And yet he couldn't quite say what was wrong.

Perhaps because they lived in the Hag's shadow, these people kept their town quiet, he thought. That might explain a lot.

"We'll sleep aboard the boat," Evann said. "If any men want to go ashore, stick together. Don't bother the locals, and don't attract attention."

Harrach stifled a yawn. "It's late. I'm going to bed, Captain."

"And I'd advise everyone else to do the same," Evann said, stretching on the deck. He pulled a pack over for a pillow.

"I think I'll take a look at those taverns," Wolfgar said slowly. Breitt and Uwe Taggart echoed his words.

"Be back before midnight," Evann growled. "Shurdan, you have first watch."

"Aye," Shurdan said, settling himself in the prow, a scabbarded sword across his knees.

*　*　*　*　*

Sleep didn't come easily for Evann. The silence grated on him. Finally he rose and stretched. A couple of hours had passed since they'd arrived. Shurdan had been relieved on watch by Harrach.

Wolfgar and the others hadn't returned yet from their tavern.

"Something wrong, Captain?" Harrach asked quietly.

"Can't sleep," he said, stretching. He still ached from his encounter with the bear. "I thought I'd get a bottle of wine. Want anything?"

"No, thanks."

Evann hopped ashore. He'd watched the others head up a narrow street, and he followed their path. The taverns would probably be in the small square he'd spotted halfway up the hillside.

Suddenly he heard footsteps to his left, coming out a narrow alley. They were heavy and seemed to drag a bit, as though the man were especially drunk. Evann stopped and sighed. Wolfgar, he thought. The man drank himself into a stupor at every opportunity.

"I do wish you'd show some sense," he began, turning.

Instead of Wolfgar, though, he found one of the villagers, an old scraggly-bearded man. Seeing Evann, the man rushed forward and grabbed the front of his shirt.

"Snakes!" he whispered. "Help me! You must stop them—*stop them snakes!*" With a hoarse gasp, he dropped to his knees and clutched at his throat. A choked gurgle came out. "*S-snakes . . .*" He fell to his side and writhed on the ground.

Evann swallowed, stepping back uncertainly. He'd seen drunks by the hundreds. He'd heard feverish men rave, and he'd watched mortally wounded men die from gaping wounds. In all his years, though, he'd never seen anything quite like this. The old man seemed to be having a seizure. And snakes? What did that mean?

"Come on," he said, stepping forward to help. "Let's get you home where you belong."

Then he saw the snakes. They appeared like a gathering fog, slowly, almost imperceptibly coming into existence. They seemed more shadow than substance, ghostly gray things, each less than a foot long, each with pale eyes that glowed in the twilight.

Gasping, Evann drew back, too shocked to run or even look away. He rubbed his eyes, thinking the snakes some illusion, some trick of the moonlight. But rather than fading like the hallucinations he believed them to be, they grew yet more substantial, more solid. He could see the scales on their backs, etched as though in glass. As he watched, they multiplied before him: they seemed to ooze from the air itself, from the buildings around them, from the man's clothing. The street filled with their writhing bodies. There were hundreds, perhaps thousands of snakes. . . .

They swarmed all over the old man now, through his hair, around his neck, over his hands and face. He opened his mouth to scream, but they poured down his throat, choking him, strangling him. His eyes rolled wildly. He clawed at his neck, hands twitching and jerking, face growing purple as he tried to breathe, but couldn't.

Evann took a step back, touching the talisman

pinned to his cloak. Fear swept through him like a sudden wind. This was magic unlike any he'd ever seen before.

The man gave a final twitch, then lay still. Dead, Evann could see. He didn't touch the body. All the snakes seemed to have vanished inside the old man.

Throwing back his cloak, he drew his sword in a quick, fluid movement, then studied the dock-side buildings. None of the villagers had appeared to help, though they must have heard the man's cries. . . . It was almost as if they'd known what would happen and didn't want to get involved. Shadows ran thick and deep in the alleys.

What did the old man say about snakes? Evann thought. That I have to stop them? He swallowed. How? He didn't have the faintest idea.

Still, he'd seen enough to know magic was involved, magic powerful enough to threaten his men and mission. He paused, listening intently. From the river, he heard small waves lapping at the docks. Wood creaked as boats shifted at their moorings. Only the tavern echoed with the sounds of men at ease. Somewhere ahead, he suddenly heard a boisterous voice—Wolfgar's, he thought—drunkenly singing.

Something scrabbled near his feet. Evann leapt back, dropping into a fighting stance. It was the old man, he saw. Somehow, impossibly, he was moving again. Evann stared, bewildered and amazed. He'd just seen this person die. He was as certain of that as he was of the snakes.

As he watched, the old man rose unsteadily to his feet. His movements were jerky and unnatural, and he held his head at an odd angle, bent up so he stared at the moon and the stars. Without a word, he turned and walked back up the alley the way he'd come.

Evann shook his head, hardly daring to believe what he'd seen. The snakes, the old man's death . . .

He ran forward and seized the old man's arm, spinning him around.

"What—" Evann began, then stopped.

The old man's eyes seethed with shadows. Nothing human remained in his blank expression. The old man jerked his arm free, turned and continued his stiff, unnatural walk through the village.

Evann backed away, whirled, and sprinted to the boat as fast as he could. He leapt to the deck.

Instantly Harrach rose, drawing his sword. "What's wrong, Captain?" he demanded.

"I saw—" Evann hesitated. What exactly *had* he seen? A few shadows, a raving old man . . . magic of some kind.

He told Harrach all that had happened.

"What did he mean?" he said. "What did I see? What were those ghostly snakes?"

Harrach cleared his throat. "I have heard legends of such things," he said, so softly Evann had to strain to hear. "I believe those snakes must be from the Shadow World, brought here to serve a dark magic."

"The Hag . . ."

Harrach leaned back. "I think that would be a safe guess, Captain—the Hag or one of her minions must control this village. Maybe even a wizard."

"A wizard . . ." Biting his lip, Evann turned and gazed ashore. "And three of my men are out there."

Suddenly loud footsteps echoed through the darkness. Evann drew his sword, then relaxed when he saw it was just Uwe Taggart. Gasping for breath, Uwe drew up short.

"Captain—" he gasped. "Wolfgar—and Breitt—"

"What about them?" Evann demanded.

"They deserted!"

"What? How?"

"I don't know!" Uwe cried.

Evann took a deep breath. More of the Hag's work, he thought.

"Start at the beginning," he said in a calmer voice. "Tell me exactly what happened."

All the other men on the boat were coming awake now. They were listening intently, though none spoke.

"I don't know what happened!" Uwe said again. "We were all of us in the tavern, drinking, and they went out to relieve themselves. And then they came back, but they were . . . different, somehow. They wouldn't talk to me. And then they just left."

"Left? You mean walked out?"

"Yes. They pretended not to know me. They

said they were fisherman!"

Evann glanced back at Harrach. "Like you said, one of the Hag's minions must be at work here. We've got to find the one responsible and stop him."

"Think of the mission, Captain," Harrach said. "Clearly the talismans don't work."

"Um . . ." said Uwe.

"What?" Evann demanded, rounding on him. "What did you leave out?"

"It was so hot inside," he said softly. "They took off their cloaks." He touched his own talisman, still pinned neatly in place.

Evann swallowed and picked up his sword. That one simple mistake might cost two men their lives, he thought.

"Harrach," he said, "you're with me. Lothar, you're in charge while we're gone. If we're not back by dawn, continue without us. You'll still have six men. That's enough."

"But, Captain—" he began, looking shocked.

"You heard my orders," Evann said firmly. Their mission to save King Graben had to come first, but he wouldn't abandon two of his men without a fight.

Lothar still looked unhappy, but he nodded.

Evann turned to Harrach. "Let's go. And pray we're not too late."

ANUIRE

eleven

From the highest window in his house, Prattis watched as Evann and Harrach left their small boat and started up the street toward the town square. Although it was dark outside, a simple spell enabled him to see everything going on below as though it were day. Now he gazed at them with a longing that made him want to rush his plans, to seize them now, before he was truly ready.

"Have patience," he whispered to himself, looking out across Gletscherel Village. "One by one, you'll have them all."

These two would be next, he decided. It would be a simple matter to grab them, remove their ridiculous protective charms, and begin the magic that would bind them to eternal servitude.

Nodding happily, he shut the window, latched it firmly, and turned toward the stairs and his workroom. It had taken great effort to possess the two sailors and the old man who had wanted to warn Evann—more effort than Prattis had used in quite a while—but rather than exhaust him, it had left him exhilarated and eager to continue.

He sighed longingly, thinking again of the Hag and how proud she would be of him. She liked nothing better than power, and he offered it.

Many years before, the king of Rzhlev had tried to arrest him for daring to explore the darker arts. He had watched from a secret room in his house while the city guard ruined half a lifetime's work—all in the space of fifteen minutes. They'd smashed his collection of rare elixirs, burned his scrolls and books, slaughtered his helpless servants before his eyes. He'd watched; he'd waited. When the guards finally left, he'd fled through the caves beneath the city.

He'd sought refuge in many temples that night, but none would take him because of the book he carried, the only thing he'd managed to save from the king's violent purge. It was the rarest object in his collection, a volume so old, scarcely a handful of men in the world still understood the language in which it had been written. He'd spent many long and lonely years trying to master it.

Ultimately, the Hag had been the only one to welcome him with open arms when he sought shelter. She had allowed him to live with her, to bask in the glow of her beauty and her power. And Prattis had been only too happy to serve.

She had give him this village to continue his work, his unholy studies, and he knew that when he mastered the arcane lore of the Shadow World, she would have no choice but to surrender herself to him, as everyone else surrendered. Then she would be his forever.

He chuckled. He had such plans for the future. Ultimately, he would return to Rzhlev. The king would bow before him. He would take the king's bloodline, and with the Hag as his queen, the world would tremble before him.

He smiled, a horrible, pinched look. Yes, it would be good to return home.

* * * * *

Harrach kicked in the tavern door, and Evann followed him in. They both had their swords drawn. Evann scowled angrily. They had no time for subtlety. Rescuing his men came first.

The people inside the tavern stared back at him with mingled fear and puzzlement.

"Where are my men?" Evann roared.

"They left," the barkeeper said softly. "They went out for a bit."

"Where did they go?"

"I don't know. I'm sure they'll be back, if you'll

wait. Do you want wine?"

"No," Evann said. He glared. "I want the truth."

The barkeeper shrugged helplessly. "I'm afraid that's all I know, sir."

Evann stepped forward and placed the tip of his sword at the man's throat. "The *truth*, I said, if you value your life!"

Blanching, the barkeeper began to stammer, "I d-don't know wh-where they w-went!"

"Feh!" Evann let him go. He seemed sincere enough, and killing him would gain them nothing. Maybe they *didn't* know anything. He looked around, searching the faces of the other men and women in the tavern. They had all drawn back a little, looking like frightened sheep.

"If they're all under the Hag's control, too . . ." Harrach whispered.

"Then they won't tell us anything." Evann nodded. "Outside," he said softly, motioning with his head. He backed out, sword held ready, but the people inside the tavern didn't try to stop them.

In the street, Evann glanced up and down. The village remained eerily quiet. Shivering a little from the cold, he tried to think. Where would a wizard be? Who could they ask?

He heard light footsteps, then a boy of perhaps eight rounded the corner at a trot, almost bumping into him. He had a basket in his arms. Leaping forward, Evann caught his arm.

"Let me go!" the boy cried, struggling to escape.

"Enough of that!" Evann said, giving him a shake. He peered at the boy more closely by the light escaping from the tavern's windows. The boy was thin, with shaggy black hair, a dirt-smudged face, and boots several sizes too big, obviously hand-me-downs from an older brother.

Evann reached into his pouch and pulled out a single silver coin. The boy's eyes bulged. He'd probably never seen so much money before.

"You want this?" he asked.

The boy looked at him, eyes wide, saying nothing.

"Well?"

"Y-Yes, sir?"

"Very well, but you'll have to earn it. Understand?"

The boy nodded.

"I seem to have gotten lost. Where does the wizard live?"

Without hesitation, the boy turned and pointed to the left, at one of the taller buildings in the next street. "That one."

Evann smiled triumphantly. Never trust a child to keep a secret, he thought. Rising, he studied the shuttered windows, the thatched roof, the tall stone walls. It seemed a gloomy enough place, especially by moonlight, and certainly suitable for a wizard. He had no doubt the child had told him the truth.

He offered the coin. The boy grabbed it and ran.

Harrach shifted uneasily beside him. "I have a bad feeling inside," he said.

"Me, too," Evann said, "but I don't see another choice. Let's get it over with."

He circled the block, with Harrach beside him, and they took to the shadows as they neared the wizard's home. Its ground floor windows had all been tightly shuttered, though a pale flickering light came from the second floor's front rooms. That had to be the wizard's workroom, he thought.

Creeping forward, he reached the front door. The handle wouldn't turn, bolted from the inside. Not a sound came from within. If not for the light on the second floor and a thin plume of smoke drifting up from the chimney and hazing the stars, he would have thought the place completely deserted.

A scraggly-bearded old man shuffled past, wheezing for breath. Evann reached out and stopped him.

"Is this where the wizard lives?" he asked.

The old man turned. It was only then that Evann recognized him as the same fisherman who'd warned him about the snakes, the fisherman who'd seemed to die. The old man's face was slack, his eyes glassy. He seemed to gaze through Evann, rather than at him.

"Wizard?" the man mumbled. "There's no wizard there. That house has been empty for as long as I can remember."

"Somebody's in it now," Evann said. "See the light?" He pointed at the second floor.

The old man barely glanced up. "Don't see anything." He started on his way again, and this time Evann didn't try to stop him.

"Curious," he murmured. "This has to be the place," he said. "Let's try around back and—"

"The talismans will protect us, Captain," Harrach said. "That's why he didn't take Uwe when he had the chance."

It made sense. Evann nodded.

"Have at it," he said.

Harrach took a step back, then charged the door. Wood splintered around the bolt. He backed up, then kicked the lock savagely. The door burst open, hinges shrieking.

"He certainly knows we're here now," Evann murmured, peering inside. The ceiling glowed with a pale yellow light, casting a sickly pall over everything.

"He knew it all the time. Don't play his games, Captain, or he's already won."

It sounded like good advice. Evann stepped forward into the entry hall. The air inside smelled musty and close, but it also held a sickly sweet tang . . . not mold or decay, exactly, but perhaps burning herbs or incense? Somehow, he'd expected something more gruesome to welcome him into this wizard's home.

Then he saw the eye. It floated, silent, unblinking, just above the door. When he turned to face it, it faded away from view. He swallowed hard.

Evann strained to hear over the wild beating of his heart and the roughness of his breath. Not a step, not a sound came from within.

"Wherever he is," Harrach said, "we'd best take care of him quickly, before he can muster his defenses."

"Cover my back," Evann said, easing forward, through a high archway into the next room.

It had once been a large dining room. A long table, covered in dust, filled the center of the room. Dust-covered wooden benches lined the walls. Above them hung faded, moldering tapestries. Other than that, the room was empty. Two small staircases led from it, one going up, the other down.

Evann glanced at Harrach. "Two staircases," he said, "one for each of us. Or perhaps we should stay together."

"Speed is more important," Harrach insisted. "We have the talismans. I think we should split up."

"Very well." Evann hesitated. He wasn't sure whether it was a good idea or not. They would find out soon enough, though. "I'll take the upstairs, then. Call if you see anything. And remember—don't kill him, not until we find the men."

"You can bet on it." Harrach headed for the down staircase.

Evann touched his talisman. He hoped it would protect him. Swallowing, he started up the broad, steep steps. Little puffs of dust rose around his boots. He kept his left hand on the wall for balance and his right hand on the hilt of his sword, ready to draw it at the first sign of trouble.

He reached the second floor and prowled through it quickly, finding little of interest. The flickering light he'd seen came from the ceiling of the front room. Whatever magic the wizard used to light his ceilings seemed to be failing there, and the light flickered faintly. The rest of the rooms contained nothing but old furniture. Evann could tell by the dust on the floor that they hadn't been disturbed in many years.

Two of the bedchambers, though, showed signs of recent habitation: one contained a large featherbed, a scattering of books and other personal effects, and crumpled piles of clothes. The other held a pair of thin pallets, perhaps for the wizard's servants.

Cautiously, he eased up the narrow, winding staircase for the third floor. On every other step, he paused and listened intently.

When he heard a slight creaking sound from above, he stopped. If anyone were going to try to ambush him, this would be the spot. Should he call Harrach? No—not yet, anyway. He didn't want to tip off whoever was waiting above. Hefting his sword, he took a deep breath and crept forward.

As soon as he stepped into the third floor hallway, two men jumped at him. Both wore loose linen clothing like the other townsfolk, and Evann felt certain he'd seen them on the dock that afternoon. Both held heavy wooden clubs.

Ducking a wild blow, Evann retreated, keeping the tip of his sword high. Fortunately, the narrowness of the hallway made it impossible for both men to face him at once.

The first fisherman moved forward, raising his club for a sharp, downward sweep.

Evann feinted, lunged, and thrust his blade through the man's chest. The fisherman looked down as if startled, and then up as the sword jerked free. He stepped forward again, seemingly uninjured, and swung his club.

It grazed Evann's arm. Cursing, Evann took a quick step back. By all rights, the fisherman should be dead now. He glanced at his sword and noticed there wasn't any blood on its blade. Swallowing, he retreated another step.

The man followed, raising his club again, and Evann slipped a knife from his belt. At this distance, he couldn't miss. He tossed it underhanded in an end-over-end roll, and it stuck in the fisherman's left eye.

The man reeled back, pawing at the knife, and managed to remove it. He made no sound. A white, milklike substance oozed from the wound.

Evann moved forward, more confident. That wound seemed to have hurt him.

Again the fisherman raised his club, but this time Evann was ready. He lunged, but instead of going for the easy chest target, he struck higher, flicking the blade across the man's one remaining eye, completely blinding him.

The fisherman dropped to his knees and began feeling his way toward Evann.

The second man pressed forward.

Drawing a second knife, Evann readied himself. Now that he knew how to hurt these people or creatures or whatever they were, it wouldn't take long to finish off these two. Then he'd go see what trouble Harrach had gotten himself into.

ANUiRE

twelve

In Grabentod, Candabraxis descended from his tower suite for the evening meal. He had taken to spending the long winter evenings in the company of the regent Harlmut, and the two of them whiled away the hours discussing the kingdom and what might be done to improve it.

At first Candabraxis had suggested trying to shift their economy back to trade and farming from piracy, but Harlmut had only shaken his head.

"It is far too late for that," he said. "We have

bred generations of warriors, not farmers, and the few farms remaining in Grabentod produce little of interest beyond the basics for life. We find it far easier to take what we want from Müden and Massenmarch and all the other kingdoms . . . and, ultimately, we find it more satisfying. Here, even our poorest enjoy fine wines, silks, and spices from around the world."

"Ah," Candabraxis had said, as if that explained it. He planned to broach the subject again when he found Harlmut in a more receptive mood. Surely something could be done to reach acceptable terms for peace with Müden.

This night, though, Harlmut wasn't waiting at the dining table. Instead, Candabraxis found him in his private office, staring into the fire with an intensity Candabraxis had seldom seen before. Clearly, the wizard thought, something had gone very wrong . . . bad news from the king, perhaps?

Gingerly he slipped into the chair next to Harlmut. He waited patiently for the regent to speak. It will all come out in good time, he thought.

"Parniel Bowspear is gone," Harlmut finally said, glancing over at him.

Candabraxis frowned. "You mean he left the city? But surely that's good news. He won't be here to undermine your rule."

"Normally I would assume so. But his ships are still in port. I can only assume he left by land."

Candabraxis leaned back and steepled his fingers thoughtfully. "You think he went after Captain Evann," he said softly.

"What else could it be?"

"How long has he been gone?"

"I don't know." Harlmut shook his head. "Several days, at least. I thought my luck too good when he seemed to be avoiding me. Now my spies say he's gone—vanished from Alber without a word. Nobody has seen him since Captain Evann left. And Bowspear has taken the best of his swordsmen along, too. At least four are gone, and probably more."

That didn't sound like good news, Candabraxis thought. But where conventional means failed, perhaps magical ones might succeed.

"I will try to locate him," he said. "Do you have anything personal of his? Some piece of clothing, perhaps, that he wore often?" He didn't know Bowspear well enough to attempt it from memory alone.

"I can get something," Harlmut said. "Why?"

"I will scry on him for you. If he *is* pursuing Captain Evann, you'll know it soon enough."

"I almost hope he is," Harlmut said. "If you can give me proof of Bowspear's treachery—real proof that no man can deny—I'll make sure he never sets foot in Grabentod again."

"Oh, it will be real enough," Candabraxis said, rising. He already knew what he needed to do . . . the spells he needed to prepare. If Bowspear truly had gone after Captain Evann, he was as good as banished.

* * * * *

An hour later, Harlmut climbed the four flights of stairs to the wizard's suite. In his hands he held an old leather boot of Bowspear's. The heel had worn down; one of his men had found it set aside for the cobbler. It had been all too easy to appropriate. Hopefully it would meet Candabraxis's requirements.

He found the door to the wizard's sitting room standing open. Through another door, he could see Candabraxis working at a table, stirring potions, grinding powders with a small mortar and pestle, and taking notes on a long piece of parchment.

"I have it!" Harlmut called.

"Come in, come in!" The wizard hurried into the sitting room to greet him. "I've finished my preparations. Is this it?" Using forefinger and thumb, he took the boot from Harlmut's hands and looked at it with distaste, giving a small sniff.

"It's the best I could do on such short notice," Harlmut said. "You said—"

"Yes, yes, it will do. Odor has nothing to do with the spell's success."

Turning, the wizard hurried back into his workroom, and Harlmut trailed him, gazing around in surprise. He hadn't been up here since Candabraxis had arrived, but he'd hardly expected such drastic changes.

The long wooden table at which he'd seen Candabraxis working dominated the room. Upon it sat an odd collection of bottles, vials, and jars. Some held thick, bubbling liquids of various colors. Others held oddly colored powders, crushed leaves, and bits of root, bark, and bones. Candles burned here and there, heating mixtures and letting off strangely aromatic scents.

In contrast, the walls bore intricate tapestries showing hunting scenes, banquets, and even a few portraits of old kings of Grabentod. Doubtless those had been provided for Candabraxis's use by one of the servants. The castle had sufficient tapestries tucked away to cover every wall several times over.

Rather than stop at the worktable, though, Candabraxis hurried around it to a clear area of the floor. There, strange diagrams had been sketched in what looked like blood. The wizard set Bowspear's boot in the center of the pattern, stood back, closed his eyes, and in a deep voice, began intoning a spell.

Harlmut felt a gathering of energy in the room, a strange crackling force that made his hair stand on end and set his teeth on edge. He shifted uneasily. He'd never been so near the creation of magic before, and it made him distinctly uneasy.

Thrice Candabraxis called Bowspear's name. The candles flickered and almost died, and a strange wind whipped around the room, fluttering the tapestries and stirring various bits of paper on the worktable.

And, just as suddenly as it had begun, the magic ended. Candabraxis sagged a little, as though exhausted. Harlmut took his elbow, steadying him.

"Well?" he asked eagerly. What had the spell

accomplished? Had he missed it? "I didn't see anything—"

Candabraxis had to lean on the worktable to catch his balance. He took a deep, cleansing breath.

"Something is shielding him," Candabraxis said softly. "It's a magic more powerful than my own scrying spell. Is there another wizard in Graben-tod who could have protected him?"

"No," Harlmut said. "You're the only wizard who's been here in generations."

Candabraxis furrowed his brow. "I don't understand, then. Where would he get such a powerful charm?"

"I think I know," Harlmut said with a grimace. So much for his hopes of finally trapping Bowspear. "He has quite a few powerful friends, including the high priestess of the Temple of Ela. If anyone could get such a charm, she could. But tell me . . . is there nothing more you can do? Can't you at least warn Captain Evann?"

Candabraxis shook his head. "I wish I could. However, the same magic that shields him from our enemies also protects him from me. . . . He is on his own until he returns."

ANUIRE

Thirteen

Harrach, for all his size and strength, could move as softly as a cat when he wanted to. He chose to now. Testing each board in the staircase before putting his full weight on it, stopping for half a minute whenever he made the slightest noise, he moved steadily downward. The wizard knew they were inside his house, but he might not know where they were.

The staircase ended at a door. Harrach pushed gently with his fingertips, and it swung silently open on well-oiled hinges. He found himself looking down a stone corridor lit by a single flickering torch. Again he crept forward.

To his right, a door stood slightly ajar. Through the narrow gap he glimpsed movement. He smiled coldly. This was what he'd been waiting for.

After taking half a step back, he kicked the door open and leapt through, brandishing his sword. A quick glance showed him the room: a chamber with bright tapestries on the walls, scattered pieces of intricately carved wooden furniture, and several tables piled high with papers. A fireplace against one wall radiated a cheerful warmth. The center of the room had been cleared, and intricate geometric designs were drawn on the floor. In the middle of the design, behind a large wooden lectern upon which perched an open book, stood a tall, gaunt, almost emaciated man with a short gray beard the same color as his robes. His head had been shaved. He barely glanced up as Harrach burst in, but kept reading from the book and mumbling to himself.

Harrach almost laughed. It would be ridiculously easy to subdue this wizard. He raised his sword and charged. One blow to knock him out, a gag and some hand restraints, and then they could worry about rendering him harmless. Old stories told of blinded, tongueless wizards who were no longer able to practice their craft. Perhaps such a fate would suit this one. . . .

Before Harrach had taken two steps, though, he felt someone grab his cloak from behind. He whirled—too late. One of the wizard's servants, hiding behind the door, ripped his cloak away in a single quiet movement.

The talisman—

The wizard stopped mumbling, looked up, and spoke a single word. Immediately Harrach found himself unable to move. His arms felt leaden, and his legs became impossibly heavy weights. Something burred like a cicada in the back of his mind.

Distantly, as though in a dream, he heard the wizard speaking to his servant. As Harrach watched in mounting terror, the man moved forward and began to bind Harrach's arms and legs with heavy ropes. The servant's fingers moved deftly, and Harrach realized he'd never be able to free himself. He had a sudden, sick feeling of despair. He couldn't even call out to warn Captain Evann.

At last, the servant finished tying him and moved away. The wizard said another word, and the heaviness on Harrach lifted. Finding himself able to move, he frantically struggled to escape.

"I'm shocked that you would disturb me," the wizard said, voice thick with the guttural accent of Rzhlev, "in the middle of a spell. Don't you know how dangerous that is? Fortunately no harm was done this time. And," he went on, watching Harrach's muscles bulge as he tried to break the ropes, "it's no use fighting. Tying knots is about the only thing my people do well. They are rather . . . *limited* in their abilities. I have not been able to teach them anything they didn't already know. But you and your captain . . . *ah!* There are so many possibilities."

"It's a trap, Captain!" he shouted as loudly as he could. "Stay back!"

The wizard laughed. "I'm afraid my men are already taking care of him. In a few minutes he, too, will be tied up. Then I'll have my time to work on you both. . . ."

Harrach glared at him. "Let me loose!"

"Do not be stupid—Harrach, is it?—and do not try to argue with me. Why should I bother when soon enough you will serve me gladly?"

He went to a table and sat, taking up a pen. Slowly, meticulous, he began to draw magical designs and patterns on a piece of parchment.

After a minute, Harrach stopped straining against the ropes. Instead, he studied the room, trying to find something, anything, to help him.

He noticed the stand on which the wizard's book rested. It was tall, graceful, made of intricately carved wood . . . an art object, designed for beauty rather than function.

He swung his legs around and struck the stand's base with his feet. It toppled easily. The wizard gave a sharp cry of dismay as his book fell into the fireplace.

Just as quickly, though, the wizard seized tongs and pulled the book from the flames. The covers were a bit scorched, the edges of the pages a bit blackened, but otherwise it appeared unhurt. The wizard sighed. He brushed it off gently, touching it like a man would touch the woman he loved.

Then he righted the book stand and moved it a more respectful distance from Harrach's feet. "You really should be more careful," he said. "Were I less benevolent of nature, I might well have killed you. However, you will serve me soon enough. Lie there calmly and wait. It won't hurt for more than a moment."

He bent over the book and began to read. The words were strange, harsh, guttural. Some seemed more sobs and wails than anything else, and all held an inflection that grated on Harrach's nerves.

Harrach began to fight desperately against the ropes. He felt something wet on his wrists and realized he'd rubbed them raw and bloody. Perhaps, he thought, the blood might let him slip loose. . . .

Still the wizard chanted. Tiny spots of black appeared in the air, each no larger in diameter than his thumb. Through them oozed ghostly, smoke-colored snakes. They seemed to writhe to the rhythm of the wizard's voice.

Then they swarmed over Harrach's body. He felt their cool, scaled hides sliding over his hands, his face, his eyes. . . .

* * * * *

Evann heard Harrach's warning cry just as he finished blinding the second fisherman. His friend was in trouble.

Backing up to the end of the hall, Evann darted forward, leapt, set foot in the middle of the first fisherman's back, vaulted the second, and found himself at the head of the staircase once more. He started down at a trot. Behind him, the two creatures fumbled their way in pursuit.

He found the second floor as empty as he'd left it, and the first floor the same, with no sign of Harrach. That meant he had to have run into trouble in the cellars below the house.

Gripping his sword more tightly, Evann eased down the staircase. Even before he reached the last step, he heard chanting from ahead. He shivered, unnerved by the liquid, throaty sounds that the voice made. It was like nothing he'd ever heard before.

Taking the torch from its holder in the wall, he moved silently toward the open door ahead. Through it he could just see Harrach's bound feet, and over Harrach swarmed the same black snakes he'd seen on the fisherman earlier that night.

No sense hesitating. Death or victory—there could be no alternative.

Plunging into the room, he found the wizard standing behind a tall, ornate lectern, reading aloud from an open book. The wizard didn't glance up, didn't stop his chant for a moment.

Evann leapt forward and brought his sword down in the crease of the open book. The blade sliced easily through the binding, shattered the lectern into so much kindling. The halves of the book flopped apart like a fish cut in two.

The wizard shrieked and dived after half of the book, trying to turn the page, trying to continue his chant uninterrupted.

Evann didn't give him a chance. He thrust the torch at the wizard's robes and set them afire.

Again the wizard shrieked, this time from pain and fear. As he tried to beat out the flames with his hands and half of the book, Evann turned to his friend.

The snakes had scattered to the corners of the room, filling the shadows with dim movement. He noticed another fisherman holding a club, but this one stood off in the corner, watching with vague indifference—waiting for orders. The wizard was too preoccupied to give any, at least for the moment.

Bending, Evann cut Harrach free. Harrach leapt to his feet, rushed to the table, and snatched up his sword and his cloak, with its protective talisman. Then he started for the wizard, face twisted with rage.

The wizard, though, had almost put out the fire. Evann seized his friend's arm and forced him toward the door, despite his protests. He had no intention of fighting both the snakes *and* their master.

"Let go of me!" Harrach roared. "I'll see him dead!"

Evann didn't. "You can't kill him," he said, "or we'll never find the others! Trust me, old friend."

Harrach tensed, as if preparing to fight, then abruptly relaxed and nodded. The bloodlust had passed. Evann let go, and Harrach fled the room.

Evann pulled the door shut and wedged the end

of the hallway torch between the door's handle
and the wall. Now that it couldn't be opened from
the inside, the wizard was trapped.

They paused and looked at each other, panting
for breath. Harrach grimaced. "What now, Captain?"

"We try to get out." He grabbed one of Harrach's bleeding wrists and looked at the wound.
The skin had been torn away in a complete circle
around the wrist. It bled freely. Evann pulled a
handkerchief from his pocket and wrapped it
around the wound, then tied it tightly to stanch
the flow of blood. Harrach winced a bit, but said
nothing. They'd both suffered worse than this before.

"Can't have your sword slipping, can we?" he
said.

As they turned for the stairs, a frantic pounding
began on the door. The wizard shouted for help
and called both their names.

Evann hesitated, glancing at Harrach. What sort
of trick was this?

"What do you want?" Harrach called to him.

"Quickly, you must let me out! The snakes! *The
snakes!*"

Evann heard a strange, half-stifled scream, followed by a thump like that of a falling body, and
then nothing more.

He had a strange, uneasy feeling, and in his
mind he could see the fisherman on the dock once
more, the snakes swarming over him, pouring
down his throat. The memory made him sick. He

wondered if that was now happening to the wizard, if he were being devoured by the shadow fiends he had summoned.

Harrach looked uneasily at him. "Do you think—?"

He nodded. "Dead by his own magic."

* * * * *

By dawn, the west wind had returned. It howled through the village, whipped down the alleys and narrow winding streets, and set the river's waves running high and choppy.

At first light, Evann burned the wizard's house. The dry wooden floors and interior walls caught at once, and flames and showers of sparks leapt high into the air, driven up like fireworks by the wind. Thick black smoke filled the sky.

Almost instantly, mourners began to fill the streets. Over half the village had suddenly and inexplicably collapsed and died: most of the adults and many of the oldest children. Evann said nothing, but knew these were the people whom the wizard had possessed with his snakes. Wolfgar and Breitt turned up dead as well. Somehow, Evann was not surprised.

The wizard's house collapsed in on itself, sending more flames shooting high into the air. The surviving villagers meanwhile wound through the streets of Gletscherel Village in a long, disorderly procession, flailing themselves with branches cut from live oak trees, trying to drive away any bad spirits still lingering in their village. Their cries were sharp and pitiful.

Swallowing, Evann led Harrach back to their fishing boat. As Uwe cast them off, Evann watched the villagers assemble on the docks. The upturned faces of men and women alike were wet with tears. They rocked back and forth, back and forth, and sobbed. Clearly, they blamed him for what had happened, and for an instant, he let himself feel guilt. If he hadn't killed the wizard, their loved ones would still be alive.

He felt a wrenching inside as he said, "Raise the sail!"

"Aye, sir!" called Harrach. The sail went up with a sudden whisper of rope and canvas, then cracked and snapped taut in the stiff breeze.

Evann forced his attention to Gletscherel Village once more. The townsfolk were staring at him. He thought of the shock and anger and betrayal they must have felt. He swallowed, feeling guilty.

"How was I to know?" he silently asked the heavens. If fate had been kind, if life could have for an instant matched the old fairy tales, the villagers might have lived on when freed from the wizard's spell. But no, such miracles would never come.

Perhaps it *would* have been better to let the wizard live, he thought for a second. He shook his head. No. It's better this way. These people, he knew deep inside, were better off dead than possessed. He only wished everyone in Gletscherel Village could understand.

He turned away, refusing to look at them any longer. Still he heard their wailing voices. The pale, pale faces of the children would haunt him for the rest of his life.

"Come on," he said to Harrach, to all the others in his suddenly grim-faced crew. They missed Lothar and Breitt as much as he did. "We still have to find Orin Hawk and save our king."

The Hag's Domain, lad? Never been there, m'self, and I reckon no sane man would go there unless he had to. It's a barren place, they say, with no people except the Hag and her minions. Aye, there's a few old towns and hunters' camps, all abandoned when the Hag took power. Sometimes the Hag uses 'em herself. Rumor says she has dozens of lairs, and that's where she hides her treasure.

What treasure? Why, the gold she takes from fool adventurers, of course. That's where she gets her gold. Aye, and I bet she takes tribute from the goblins and the orogs and the trolls in her mountains, too. They all know better than to take her on!

What else is there? Well, forests and mountains, a lake or two, and lots of snakes—the Hag has a particular kinship with snakes, I hear. They answer her when she calls. She's half snake herself, ye know. . . .

ANUIRE

fourteen

More snow had fallen in the Drachenaur Mountains than in Grabentod, Parniel Bowspear found as he led his men up the Warde Pass. He had to keep an eye on the ground at all times to avoid slipping.

The mountains rose to either side of them, steep and rocky, with only the occasional gnarled, leafless tree or tuft of grayish grass to break the otherwise barren landscape. Though only an inch or so of snow lay on the ground here, it spoke of trouble to come if a larger storm hit. Bowspear glanced for the dozenth time at the sky, as clear and blue and cloudless as he'd ever seen, but he'd experienced quite enough storms at sea not to trust the weather to hold.

Pausing, he sucked in a deep lungful of air. His breath misted before him, forming ice crystals that he had to keep brushing out of his beard. The thin, cold air felt like knives when be breathed through his nose.

Now came the dangerous part. They would have to prepare an ambush for Captain Evann while staying warm and dry and eluding the Hag, not to mention the other denizens of this inhospitable realm. Unfortunately, the Warde Pass seemed increasingly a bad choice for their ambush; it offered no place to hide, and little cover.

No, he thought, we will have to keep going. Perhaps we will find a suitable place when we turn off into the smaller pass to that old abandoned logging camp—Zwei Frieren Flusse.

He glanced over his shoulder. His men had strung out into a long line, perhaps ten yards between each one. He had taken the lead that morning, setting a swift pace, but they had all managed to keep up without incident. Unfortunately, with fresh snow on the ground, they left ample tracks, but he could do nothing about it now. Perhaps Evann would think orogs or goblins had passed through ahead of him.

The path opened up onto a broad ledge. They would all be able to rest here. Raising one hand, he signaled a halt. Everyone caught up and formed a circle around him.

"We're going to have to move more carefully," he said, looking each in the eye. "We're on the edge of the Hag's Domain now."

Their faces remained impassive. Good; they weren't intimidated. He'd picked them well.

"Yuri," he went on, "you're on scout duty. See what's ahead. We'll follow about a hundred yards back. Don't shout a warning—signal it. No telling what might hear you here, and we don't want to start an avalanche from above."

"Aye, sir," Yuri said. He glanced up the slopes toward the ice and snow far above, as if expecting it to suddenly fall on him, then turned and headed up the pass. It wound sharply to the right and vanished behind the mountain.

Counting slowly to a hundred, Bowspear watched him go. When he was certain Yuri was far enough ahead, he started after him.

"Stay close behind me," he cautioned the others.

It would take them at least two days to get through to the smaller pass to Zwei Frieren Flusse, he knew. He'd heard of a few small caves that travelers used for shelters along the way. They'd look for one tonight.

As the day wore on and he trudged ever onward through the cold, Bowspear found his thoughts wandering to what might lie ahead of them in the pass. There were many possible dangers here. Though orogs and goblins were almost never seen in Grabentod, folk stories told of them teeming in the mountains, sometimes sneaking down by night to kidnap unsuspecting children.

He had never been this far into the mountains before. Several times, he had accompanied King Graben to his hunting lodge on Mount Krakenwald, but the only dangers in that part of the Drachenaur Mountains came from wildlife, avalanches, and occasional forest fires. Here, though . . . here he half expected to find monsters lurking around every bush or bend.

He almost wished he'd stayed in Grabentod. What chance could Captain Evann possibly have of success here, against the elements, the creatures who lived in the mountains, and the Hag herself? Here, facing the mountains, he felt an almost oppressive sense of impending disaster.

Yuri came jogging back, half slipping on the snow and patches of ice. Drawing up short, Bowspear waited, hand dropping to his sword. His scout didn't seem upset or alarmed by anything, probably just coming back to give a routine report.

"What is it?" he asked.

Yuri panted a moment, hands on knees, catching his breath. "Sir," he said, "we're coming up on the pass to Zwei Frieren Flusse."

"Any sign of a lodge or a camp where we can spend the night?"

"No, sir," he said.

Bowspear nodded. "Very well. We'll see how far we can make it before nightfall."

Yuri gave a nod, turned, and headed back up the pass. Bowspear resumed his slow march.

As the party rounded the right side of another immense mountain, Bowspear abruptly found himself on a wide stone ledge. A low, moaning wind came up, numbing his fingers and making his eyes sting. To the left, a steep cliff dropped away several hundred feet into a deep gorge. A dark, stagnant-looking lake, half iced over, sat at the bottom.

Keeping as close to the mountain as he could, Bowspear pressed on, every now and again catching sight of Yuri far ahead. The rock underfoot felt icy and slick beneath the snow, and Bowspear almost fell several times.

Suddenly he rounded a corner and came to where the pass split. One trail—broader than the first—continued to the left toward Drachenward. The other, smaller pass climbed steeply and wound out of sight. It looked little better than a goat trail. It had to be the one to Zwei Frieren Flusse and the Hag's Domain.

Standing at the top of the smaller pass, Yuri turned and waved them on, and then he vanished out of sight, following the trail downward.

Tucking his head into the wind, Bowspear picked his way forward. He climbed the smaller pass, using his hands to pull himself up. A stone twisted unexpectedly under his heel, but he managed to catch his balance before he fell. If he broke his leg, he'd be stranded and die.

At last, he reached the top of the pass. There he paused to catch his breath, get his bearings, and give the rest of his men a hand up. Ahead, the smaller pass leveled out again and turned into what appeared to be a long-abandoned road. An avalanche must have blocked the road some years before, and he and his band had just climbed to the top of the fallen rock and debris.

From this vantage point, shading his eyes, Bowspear could follow the road's course for several miles ahead. In places, it had been obliterated entirely by passing centuries, but then it picked up again. Looking down on it from above, the road looked like a long gray stone ribbon.

It would make their passage easier, he thought, but it might well be watched. Bowspear considered the possibilities for a long moment before deciding to press on as before. There didn't seem to be much alternative. With Yuri scouting ahead, at least they would have warning of any dangers.

Bowspear picked his way down to where the road began. By the time he reached the bottom, he found Yuri scrambling back, an alarmed expression on his face.

"What is it?" he demanded in a soft voice.

"Goblins," Yuri said. "Two of them, sitting in the mouth of a cave. They're guards, I think."

Slowly, Bowspear nodded. It made sense. Goblins wouldn't want humans invading their territory any more than humans wanted them invading Grabentod. He glanced up the pass, then back the way they'd come. There didn't seem to be much choice, he thought. They'd have to go up the side of the mountain, work their way above the goblins, then descend to the road on the other side. If they kept to cover and didn't start any rock slides, he thought they'd be able to make it in an hour or two. That wouldn't leave much time before dark, but perhaps it would get them to safety.

He told Yuri his plan. "See if it's passable over there," he said, pointing up over the goblins' cave.

Yuri gave a quick nod and began scrambling up the steep slope. Ice and shale skittered out from under his boots, but the noise vanished in the wind. A hundred fifty feet up, Yuri found a ledge where he could stand. He scouted ahead a bit, then returned and motioned everyone to follow him.

Bowspear climbed after him. One by one, the rest of his men followed. At last, exhausted, he pulled himself up onto the ledge. It was perhaps three feet wide here and seemed to run a good way ahead. This might be just what they needed to get around the goblin sentries. Unfortunately, they had less than an hour of sunlight left. They weren't going to make it through the pass tonight.

"Nakkar," he said, pulling the next men up, "I want you to go carefully, but catch up with Yuri. Tell him to start looking for a place we can camp tonight. We're not going to make it out of here by dark."

"Sir!" Nakkar gave him a quick salute, then stalked cautiously down the ledge toward where Yuri stood.

Bowspear helped the next man up onto the ledge, keeping an eye on Yuri and Nakkar as they talked. He wished he could hear what they were saying, but the rising wind swept their words away.

At last Yuri turned toward Bowspear, pointed down and a little to the left, and pantomimed an opening. Another cave? Or just an alcove where they might shelter for the night? After a moment's hesitation, Bowspear motioned for him to check it out.

He pulled the last of his men up. Gratefully, he rested with the others, all sitting on their haunches and puffing.

Bowspear turned and gazed expectantly toward the last place he'd seen Yuri. His scout had vanished. Leaning out over the ledge, Nakkar peered down at something . . . probably the cave, Bowspear thought.

Suddenly an inhuman scream cut through the air. Bowspear jumped, startled, and then turned and raced down the ledge. Nakkar was shouting and pointing, but Bowspear couldn't make out the words. Something about a fight?

Not more goblins, Bowspear prayed.

"What is it?" he demanded as he reached Nakkar's side.

Nakkar swallowed nervously. "Something grabbed Yuri and pulled him in!"

"Something?" Bowspear demanded. "What kind of something? A goblin? An orog?"

"I—I don't know! Whatever it was, it was huge!"

Bowspear leaned out to see for himself. Twenty feet below, he spotted the tall, narrow cave Yuri had been investigating. As he watched, Yuri's head rolled out of the cave, bounced several times down the mountainside, and vanished from sight below.

Bowspear felt sick. Yuri had been with him nearly five years now, and he'd never had a more loyal follower. What could have beheaded him? Goblins?

No, not goblins, he realized a moment later. A huge, hairy creature three times as tall as a man pulled itself out from the cave's mouth. It held the trunk of a small tree in one hand as a club. Slowly it scanned the slope below its cave. Then it turned, saw Bowspear and Nakkar, and with a roar of anger started climbing toward them.

"Crossbows!" Bowspear shouted to his men, drawing his sword. Turning, he fled back along the ledge.

Nakkar was scrambling farther up the side of the mountain, a horrified, panicked expression on his face. The creature—a rock troll, Bowspear guessed, though he'd never seen one before—rapidly closed the distance between them. It was making a low animal grunting noise deep in its throat.

Nakkar wasn't going to make it.

"Draw your sword!" Bowspear shouted into the wind. "It's almost on you!"

Nakkar glanced down and saw the troll. Abruptly, he dived to the left, rolling down the mountain and across the shale. Loose stones cascaded down the slope, and then Nakkar landed on the ledge, bounced, and started to slide off. He just managed to grab the edge, where he clung desperately.

Giving another roar, the troll began climbing back down to the ledge.

Bowspear reached his men and saw they had their crossbows ready. They'd been waiting for Nakkar and him to get clear.

"Fire!" Bowspear shouted, diving forward and flattening himself on the ledge.

Bolts flew over him. Two missed the troll's head narrowly, and it swung around, swatting at them as if they were insects. The third struck it in the arm, and the fourth hit it a glancing blow to the neck.

Enraged, it lifted its tree-club over its head. In one movement, it threw the log at Bowspear and his men. Luckily the club dropped a few yards short, skidded off the ledge, and fell, rolling down the mountain.

"Reload and fire at will!" Bowspear shouted.

His men were already doing that. Two more bolts flew, both catching the troll in the chest. It stood erect, clawing at its chest, making a futile pained sobbing sound. Another bolt hit it, this one glancing off its right temple. A spatter of blood flew, and the creature toppled backward. It slid off the ledge and vanished from sight.

Bowspear found his legs weak. He wanted to sit down and catch a second wind, but knew he had to do something about Nakkar. The man still clung to the ledge.

Though weak in the knees, Bowspear forced himself back onto his feet, hurried forward, and grabbed Nakkar's arm. Slowly he hauled him up to safety. Nakkar lay still, gasping for air like a fish out of water. Cuts and bruises covered his face, hands, and arms.

Bowspear opened his pack, rummaged through it to find the flask of brandy he'd brought, and put it to Nakkar's lips. The man took a few gulps, and that seemed to steady his nerves. He sat up and gave a weak grin. "I made it, sir."

"Poor Yuri," Bowspear murmured. He'd thought there might be casualties, but he'd never suspected they would come so soon. Yuri was a good man, leaving behind a young widow.

He shrugged on his pack again. With darkness almost upon them, they still had to get under cover. At least they'd have a place to spend the night, thanks to Yuri. Hopefully it wouldn't be too foul.

"Let's get moving," he said. "We still have to lay poor Yuri to rest."

* * * * *

It took them half an hour to make it safely down to the opening of the cave. Bowspear insisted on slow, careful progress. If the troll they'd killed had a mate, he didn't want to lose any more men to her.

By the time they reached the cave's mouth, the sun had begun to disappear behind the peaks.

Bowspear paused, listening over the moan of the wind, but heard nothing from within. Cautiously, he stepped inside.

The smell hit him first, a deep musky stench of excrement and rotting meat. Truly, the troll's cave was the most ghastly place he had ever been before. The floor was covered with half-gnawed bones, and a few of them still had flesh attached. They had to be from goblins, he thought, noting how thick they were.

The troll had evidently made this his lair for many years. Rocks had been piled in the front opening, closing it up to what must have been a narrow passage for the troll, though two men could have passed through it shoulder to shoulder.

"There's Yuri," Nakkar said softly, pointing to one corner.

Bowspear squinted and could just make out a headless form there, tossed aside like a child's doll, a broken, lifeless heap. Swallowing, covering his nose against the stench, he moved forward, grabbed Yuri's arm, and began to drag him to the ledge. He didn't deserve to be left in here, forgotten amid the countless bones of goblins, Bowspear thought. They'd build a stone cairn for him on the ledge outside.

After a second's hesitation, the others moved to help. It was the least they could do for their friend.

As he stepped out of the troll's cave, though, a guttural voice called, "Hold there!" and he felt the sharp tip of a spear thrust up against his spine.

ANUIRE

fifteen

The goblins marched Bowspear and his men around the side of the mountain to another cave. Disarmed, outnumbered, he still watched and waited for his chance to escape. If even the slightest opportunity presented itself, he planned on taking it.

Unfortunately, none came. The thirty-five goblins who'd captured them—short, gnarled, grayskinned creatures in crude armor, with spears and axes constantly held ready—kept a close and careful guard.

As they passed through the cave mouth and into a broad stone passageway curving down and to the right, Bowspear noted hundreds of goblin faces leering out at him from side passages. Many of them gnashed their teeth, making horrible grinding noises. Others hooted in glee.

"Keep goin'!" grunted one of the goblins behind Bowspear, shoving him in the small of the back.

Bowspear stumbled, almost falling, but quickened his pace. No sense getting hurt in a fight with the guards. He and his men would need all their strength if they were going to escape.

At last they reached a broad underground cavern lit by smoky torches. More goblins joined the procession, surrounding them, and still they were herded on. Bowspear watched their faces, but saw little sympathy.

At last, the march halted before a blacksmith. Coal burned a deep orange-red in his forge, and the thick black smoke drifted slowly upward. Bowspear covertly glanced at the ceiling. The smoke seemed to be floating up into a natural chimney. If they could break away and climb inside it, they might well escape.

The blacksmith, a burly goblin covered in soot, began selecting heavy iron chains from a rack.

"You!" one goblin said, pointing to Nakkar.

Nakkar gulped.

Grinning wickedly, the goblin guard prodded him toward the blacksmith. Nakkar leapt away from the jabbing spear point.

Seizing his arms, the blacksmith fastened huge

iron manacles to his wrists, then chained them to shackles on his feet. Clinking a bit, Nakkar returned to the line. He could barely move, Bowspear saw with rising panic. If they didn't do something now, they wouldn't get a chance.

"I want to see your leader," Bowspear demanded suddenly, stepping forward. "I'm a man of importance."

The blacksmith laughed. An old, grizzled goblin with a huge scar across half his face stepped forward, looking Bowspear over carefully. In one quick movement, he ripped Bowspear's shirt off his back, then circled him, feeling his muscles. Bowspear tensed, angered and outraged, but he knew better than to fight.

"Good eating," the goblin announced with a grin.

A horrible sick jolt ran through Bowspear. So that was to be their fate . . . eaten by goblins in the mountains.

He swallowed and once more glanced up at the natural chimney. *So close . . .*

* * * * *

Captain Evann pulled his gray woolen cloak more closely about himself and tried not to shiver. The wind felt bitterly cold here, on the water, as they sailed up the Gletscherel. They were rounding a bend, and ahead he heard the roar of a waterfall.

Gradually Gletscherel Felsen came into sight,

and the size and beauty of it caught him by surprise. The falls stretched easily two hundred feet across, tumbling off a high rocky cliff in a dazzling show of froth and foam. The sun caught the spray, casting a huge bright rainbow across the sky, and the air smelled fresh and moist. Evann didn't think he had ever seen anything quite so amazing before. If it weren't for the Hag, surely a village would have sprung up here long ago.

All his men were chattering excitedly. He found he didn't blame them. It took effort to tear his gaze away from the falls.

Studying the shore, he decided to land on a small rocky bank just to the left of the falls. They could beach their craft there. If the fishermen returned to claim it, it would be safe enough. If not . . . they might be able to use it on their way back. He nodded. A good plan.

"Put in there," he said, pointing.

"Aye, sir," Harrach called from the rudder.

As soon as he heard their hull scrape bottom, Evann leapt to shore from the prow. As Uwe lowered the sail and Harrach lashed the rudder down, everyone else stripped off boots and pants and, in just undergarments, hopped out knee- or thigh-deep into the icy water. Quickly they dragged the boat up out of the water.

"Gather wood and light a fire," Evann said. "Dry yourselves off. I'm going to take a quick look around."

As the men hurried to obey, Evann headed for the cliffs beside the falls. There has to be a way to the top, he thought, tilting his head back and studying them. He'd heard of an old trade pass here.

As he neared the cliff, the roar of the falls grew deafening, and a cold spray fell like a mist on his face and hands. Then he spotted a narrow, winding path carved deep into the rock. It had been carefully disguised to look like part of the mountain, and it led all the way to the top.

Nodding, he returned to find his men clustered around a small fire, busily toweling themselves off with cloths taken from the fishing boat. They were using dry wood, so the fire didn't let off much smoke, but it wouldn't do to have it burning more than they needed.

Evann fetched a bucket from the boat, filled it with water, and hauled it back to them. As the last of them finished dressing, he emptied the bucket on the flames. Hissing and sizzling, the fire went out.

"I found the pass," he said, shouldering his pack. "Follow me. Keep close together, and watch your step—it's slick from the spray."

Turning, he led the way to the path. As he'd expected, it proved readily accessible—a long, stepped climb, full of turnings and switchbacks. The rock underfoot, slick and icy, proved a little treacherous, but the company made the climb with few slips and no falls.

As they reached the top, Evann glanced back and down. Below, nestled in the little river valley, sat their boat. From this height it looked more like some child's lost toy than a sailing vessel. The Gletscherel itself swept on, curving between the mountains on either side and vanishing from sight.

He drew a deep breath and turned. Onward, he thought. Winding gently to the left, the river passed through a dense forest of towering pines. Along its bank grew waist-high grass, now brown and dead with winter fast approaching.

Few people had come this way in generations, Evann realized. He walked toward the riverbank, shoving his way through the grass, feeling like an explorer venturing into the wilderness. He saw no signs of logging or camps, no tracks or trails that hadn't been made by small game. The scruffy waist-high brown grass ahead of them showed no sign of ever having been trampled down by anyone passing through.

At last Evann reached the soft muddy bank. The river had cut a deep path here over the centuries, and the low winter water level left ten feet clear. They would have no trouble making their way.

On the other side of the river, directly across from the company, three deer looked up from drinking, then bolted into the cover of the trees, white tails flicking. A few birds called raucously from the pines. Then came silence, broken by only the muted roar of the falls behind them.

Despite how safe it looked, Evann had to remind himself that this was the Hag's Domain. He started forward, skirting just short of the water in the clearest passage. Though the land around them looked deserted, it likely held any number of traps, as had the village where they had run into the wizard.

Squinting up at the sun, Evann guessed the time at just after noon. Another hour, he thought, and they would stop for a rest and a quick meal.

Taking a deep breath, he checked his sword, then pressed onward.

* * * * *

The day proved singularly uneventful, which pleased Evann. The most danger they encountered was a brown bear, but this one showed no interest in them and ambled away even as they approached.

Toward evening, they passed completely through the forest and onto a small grassy plain. Ahead lay a large lake, the origin of the Gletscherel, and on its shore, jutting up from the grass, he could see the scattered stone walls and chimneys of a ruined settlement. There were only fifteen or twenty houses, and they looked as though they had been abandoned for decades.

Evann hesitated. Darkness had almost overtaken them, and he hadn't relished the idea of spending the night out under the stars. Here, on the plain, an open fire would be visible for miles in all directions.

Harrach moved up beside him. "What do you think, Captain?" he asked.

"It may be a good place to shelter," Evann said

slowly. "On the other hand, some of the Hag's creatures might well inhabit the ruins."

"Shall I check them out?"

"Aye," Evann said. "Take Freisch and Uwe with you. Be careful . . . keep everyone in sight at all times."

"You heard the captain," Harrach called to the others. He shrugged off his pack and drew his sword, and Uwe and Freisch did the same.

"Give a shout if you see anything," Evann said.

The three of them spread out in a line, advancing on the village. Evann watched as they carefully ventured among the ruins. Several times, he tensed as he lost sight of one or two of them, but they always reappeared.

Nor did they seem to find anything lurking in the ruins. He relaxed a bit as Harrach sheathed his sword, called something to Uwe and Freisch, and the three of them jogged back to join him.

"Nothing there but stone," Harrach reported, panting a little. "I think we'll be safe enough tonight."

"Good." Evann found his mood brightening a little. He hadn't been looking forward to spending a night in the open in the cold. Dusk had started to fall, and with it came a cold breeze off the lake.

Shouldering his pack, Harrach led the way. Evann looked around curiously as they entered the ruins. The buildings seemed to have been abandoned voluntarily; he saw no sign of char marks on the stone to show the inhabitants had been burned out. They might well have fled when the Hag took up residence here; the buildings were old enough.

Harrach said, "I think we're best off in here for the night." He indicated a large building in the center of the village. It had the highest standing walls. "Someone camped here—there's still a fire circle in the middle and some of the wood they scavenged from the ruins."

"When?" Evann ducked through the low doorway. Though the roof had long ago fallen in, it seemed a good enough place to spend the night. The walls would also shelter them from the wind and provide some cover for a campfire.

"At least a year," Harrach said, following him inside.

"Ah." The large circle of stones in the center of what had been the main room held a few gray smudges and half-burned logs. "Probably some of the Hag's men on patrol, perhaps even Orin Hawk."

"Perhaps," Harrach agreed.

The others came in and threw down their packs. Without a word, Uwe set about laying a fire, kindling it with dry grass he'd carried in. Striking sparks with his flint and steel until one of them caught, he leaned forward and blew softly on the tiny ember, feeding it more grass and splinters of wood. Finally it caught fire, and he started piling on the wood that the ruins' previous visitors had left stacked in one corner.

Evann sat with his back up against one wall, staring into the flames and thinking back to Wolfgar and Breitt, dead before they had halfway reached their goal. It would be a long, long journey yet to come.

"I'll take first watch," he said. "Freisch, you'll have second, then Turach, then Uwe, then Harrach. Eat, then get some rest. We'll leave at dawn."

Everyone else seemed to share his dark mood. As the fire warmed the ruins, they stretched out their bedrolls, ate trail rations, and stared into the flames or the sky, now full of stars. Slowly, one by one, all but Evann curled up in their blankets and fell asleep.

Rising, he put a couple more logs on the fire, then went to the doorway and gazed out across the lake. It glimmered faintly in the moonlight, low waves rippling with silver. Around him the wind made a low moan as it whipped around the old stone walls, hummed down ancient chimneys, or slid catlike through gaping doors and windows. He shivered a bit, wondering about the people who had lived here.

Suddenly he heard what sounded like a footstep to the left, outside the building. Whirling, he drew his sword, ready to give a cry of warning.

It wasn't a soldier, though. It was a woman in a long, flowing white dress, with a veil across her face. Her eyes glimmered like blue diamonds, and she stretched pale arms toward him.

"Terrill," she whispered, "come to my, my love."

Powerless to stop himself, Captain Terrill Evann put down his long sword and walked into her cold, cold embrace.

ANUIRE

sixteen

The morning of his fifth day in Grabentod, Candabraxis rose with the sun, threw open the shutters of his room, and breathed in the cold, crisp air. It felt good to be alive, he thought, gazing down on the city below.

His journey, and then the forced use of so much magic at once, had left him exhausted. Although he had gone through the motions that polite conversation and society demanded, his heart had not truly been in them. Now, though . . . now, he felt like exploring the city. He still had a mystery to solve: why *had* Grabentod called to him when he was at sea?

The fishing boats had already left port, and several of the roundboats were missing—doubtless off on some new raid—but still the city bustled with life. Market day had arrived. In the largest square, some merchants had spread brightly colored blankets on the flagstones to display their wares. Others had set up little stands or booths, and still others had pens or cages for livestock. Children darted here and there, men and women shopped, and barkers hawked their goods in voices that carried faintly even as far as the castle.

Candabraxis smiled. It had been a long time since he'd been to market. This would give him a chance to see more of the city, meet some of the people, and see if he could find answers to his questions.

Shuttering his window to the cold, he washed up quickly, put on loose gray pants and a white linen shirt with laces up the front, which the castle's tailor had provided for him, and threw on his heaviest wool cloak. Then, taking a small pouch of coins from his chest, he descended to the ground floor. He'd find something to eat at the market. His stomach rumbled hungrily.

By the time he reached the market square, the happy bustle had grown to a crushing throng. Half of Alber had turned out, it seemed. He squeezed past a pair of women carrying huge baskets of bread, ducked under the bundle of reeds a man carried past on his shoulder, and stepped around a line of five goats being herded past by a pair of young boys.

Everywhere, bedlam ruled. Merchants haggled with customers, sheep and goats and chickens *baa*ed or bleated or clucked, and people jostled one another in their haste to get by.

Candabraxis eventually made his way to the center of the square, where a large platform stood. Here he found half a dozen servants he recognized from the castle. They were all selling goods at a brisk pace from long wooden tables.

Stepping forward, he picked up a beautiful green silk scarf. It had small red emblem stitched in one corner . . . the sign of the House of Krael. It had come from the Merchant Edom's ship.

Swallowing, he put it back. He wanted no part of stolen goods, and especially not stolen from his friend Edom. This must be how King Graben disposed of loot he didn't keep; Harlmut had mentioned tithes from Bowspear on the day he'd arrived.

"I'll give ye a good price on that," said one of the servants behind the counter. "Real silk, that is—comes from worms in Avanil, I hear."

"Silk worms, yes," murmured Candabraxis. "I was just looking."

His stomach growled again, and he turned and wandered from the booth, following the scent of frying sausages and breads. He reached a line of booths selling food: warm meat pies, beers and ales, and all manner of pastries. Perhaps a small mince pie would hit the spot.

As he reached for his pouch, he felt something hit him hard in the side. A knife blade slashed past. Suddenly his pouch flopped open, spilling coins across the cobblestones with loud jingling noises. The edge of the blade just nicked his palm.

Instantly Candabraxis whirled, flinging his cloak into his attacker's face. He began a quick charm spell, but the man blundered away from him, throwing off the cloak and running.

Candabraxis let the spell dissipate, uncast. He hadn't reacted quickly enough . . . or his attacker had reacted too quickly. His hand suddenly ached with a sharp, cold, probing pain, and he glanced down in alarm. Already, that minor cut had begun to swell, and it now bulged out in a lump the size of a small lemon. Quickly, he retrieved his cloak and wrapped his hand. There had been something on the blade, poison or some spell. He'd have to get back to his tower and see what could be done about it.

Around him, people were patting him on the back sympathetically and saying things about having to watch out for cutpurses and pickpockets. Others, including a few children, were helping gather up his coins. For a people of pirates and cutthroats, he thought ironically, they were strangely honest.

The pain in his hand grew more intense, pulsing up his arm and shooting into his shoulder. He cried out in sudden agony. Then everything started to go dark, and he felt himself falling.

* * * * *

When the servant burst into his sitting room, Harlmut caught his breath in sudden fear. For months now, he'd been half expecting Bowspear to barge in and kill him in the middle of the night. He relaxed only when he recognized Jarick, one of the few loyal men he had left.

"Sir," Jarick said, gasping for breath, "the wizard—he's been stabbed in the market!"

"What?" Harlmut leapt to his feet. "When? Who did it?"

"Less than an hour ago. The man got away—"

"And Candabraxis?"

"We brought him to his tower. I think he's dying!"

Harlmut swallowed. Stabbed . . . that sounded like Bowspear's work. Perhaps it wouldn't be as bad as Jarick said. Servants had a tendency to exaggerate.

"What about the healer?" he demanded.

"Pfeiran went to fetch her."

Harlmut nodded. Mari was a good, sturdy woman who cared nothing for politics and much for the healing arts. If anyone could save the wizard, she could.

"Get back to the tower," he ordered. "Stay with the wizard until I get there. Don't let anyone near him except Mari."

"Yes, sir." Bobbing his head, Jarick fled the sitting room.

Frowning, a thousand fears running through him, Harlmut pulled on his boots, threw on a cloak, and ran for the tower. If he could do anything to save his friend, he'd do it.

* * * * *

Mari had already arrived by the time Harlmut reached the wizard's side. Candabraxis lay in his bed, pale as death, his eyes closed, taking rapid, shallow breaths, almost gulping the air. Sitting on a small stool beside him, she worked quickly and methodically.

She had already cut off his shirt and tied a tourniquet around his right arm. Harlmut stared, a little sick at his stomach, at the wizard's right hand. Black as coal and veined with dark purplish lines, it had swollen to three times its normal size. It had also begun to give off a foul, almost putrid smell, like that of rotting flesh.

"What caused this?" he asked softly.

"Two things, poison and magic," Mari said. "The poison can be stopped easily enough with borstice root. The magic . . . ah, there is the hard part. Hush, now, and let me work."

Swallowing, Harlmut drew up a chair and sat beside her.

"Bring a jar and a candle," she said. "Hold them for me."

Harlmut hurried into the next room. Several large jars sat on the wizard's worktable. He up-ended one, dumping out a small pile of dried leaves. Clutching that and a candle, he hurried back to the healer's side.

Without a word Mari took the jar. She picked up a small, thin-bladed knife, passed it twice through the candle's flame, then reached out and slit the wizard's hand from thumb tip to heel.

Harlmut cried out in alarm as dozens of small, white worms tumbled from the wound. Mari caught them all in the jar. Then, like a woman squeezing the juice from an orange, she began squeezing his arm just below the tourniquet, forcing more worms out into the jar.

When she finished, she handed the jar to Harlmut. "Burn them," she said.

Harlmut gazed down at the white, writhing mass inside the jar. They weren't worms at all, he realized, and his horror grew. They were tiny white snakes. He could see their little tongues flicking out, and little blood-red eyes stared up at him with what seemed to be a cold, cruel intelligence.

Shuddering, he carried them into the wizard's workroom. There he found a small unlit oil lamp. After pouring the oil into the jar, on top of the snakes, he touched a candle to them. The oil caught fire at once, and the snakes burned, making a shrill hissing noise. A foul black smoke roiled up from the jar.

Harlmut crossed to the window, threw open the shutters, and set the jar on the ledge, still burning. The smoke streamed up into the sky.

He returned to find Mari dressing the wizard's wounded hand. She had released the tourniquet, and Candabraxis's arm had regained a little of its fleshy color. At least it isn't black anymore, Harlmut thought. He'd been afraid Mari would have to amputate the limb.

"Lucky for him they cut only his hand, and it only a little," Mari said. Clucking a bit to herself, Mari pushed and prodded the wizard's hard, flat stomach with her fingers, feeling his inner organs.

"A *little?*" Harlmut said, aghast.

"Aye, a slice no larger across than your little finger. If that blade had cut him on his side or chest, he'd be long dead, eaten from the inside out."

Harlmut gave a shudder. "But he'll be all right now?"

"I said no such thing. Ah! What have we here?"

Candabraxis shifted, moaning deeply as she prodded his left side. Then he produced a series of racking wet coughs that set Harlmut's skin crawling.

"In my bag I have a pair of knitting needles," Mari said. "Fetch one. I will need your help, Harlmut, if we're to save him."

"Anything," he said, rising. What could she possibly use knitting needles for?

He found them, along with a skein of yarn, inside the bag she'd brought. Selecting one of the needles, he brought it back to her.

"You must hold him down," she said, placing one of his hands on each of the wizard's shoulders. "This will hurt him, and he will struggle. Keep him down, or it will mean his death. Understand?"

"Yes, Mari," he said.

Keeping her fingers on his stomach, just below his ribs, she picked up her knife again, passed it through the candle's flame, and then, in one swift motion, cut a two-inch incision.

Candabraxis shrieked in agony and tried to arch his back. Harlmut put all his weight on the wizard's shoulders and pushed him down.

Mari, moving so quickly he almost missed it, snatched up her knitting needle, jabbed it into the wound, hooked something, and pulled.

Slowly a long white tail emerged from the hole. She continued to pull, and six inches, then a foot, then a foot and a half of snake emerged. The snake's tail began to lash, whipping back and forth. It wrapped itself around Mari's wrist and tightened.

Candabraxis screamed again as the snake's head came free of his body. Holding its head firmly between thumb and forefinger Mari took her knife and drove the blade through the creature's brain. The snake gave a long, low hiss as it died.

Mari held the white corpse out to Harlmut. "Burn it," she said simply.

The wizard had stopping struggling, so Harlmut let go and gingerly took the snake's body. It felt warm as blood and soft as a baby's skin. Gingerly, he carried it into the workroom, cut it into several pieces, and dropped them one by one into the still-burning jar on the windowsill. Then he added more oil to make sure all the snakes burned away to nothing.

By the time he got back to the wizard's side, Mari had finished dressing the new wound on his stomach. She pulled the blankets up around his chin and tucked him in like a mother would her firstborn child.

"There now," she murmured. "Sleep for old Mari. You'll be up again before you know it."

It seemed to Harlmut that Candabraxis began to smile a little. A healthy flush had returned to the wizard's cheeks, and he breathed deeply and regularly again.

Softly, Harlmut drew Mari aside. He didn't quite know what had happened, but he knew it was evil. He couldn't allow such magic in Grabentod.

"Those snakes," he began.

The old healer shook her head. "A foul magic," she said. "My grandmother saw it once, long ago. Her patient died before she found out what caused it. My mother saw it twice, but both times she arrived too late to help." Mari glanced sidelong at the wizard. "This one, he was lucky."

"Do you have any idea who caused it?"

She hesitated. "It is not my place to guess at blame."

"Please, we may all be in danger."

"My grandmother, she knew who killed hers: an assassin sent in the dark of night by the Night Walkers."

Haltengabben, Harlmut thought, could easily arrange an assassination if she wanted to. And yet he had no proof . . . no proof that Haltengabben and Bowspear were allies, no proof that Haltengabben had sent an assassin to kill Candabraxis, no proof of anything.

At least the wizard had survived. Perhaps he could identify the man who had attacked him.

"Will you stay with him?" he asked Mari.

"Tonight, yes. But keep a watch over us both— guards you trust at the door. And I must prepare all his meals personally tomorrow. His stomach will be weak, and he needs certain herbs to speed his healing."

"Agreed," he said quickly. "And . . . thank you."

"Do not thank me so quickly," she said, eyeing him darkly. "We all pay a price for help we request."

ANUIRE

seventeen

Bowspear lay still in the dark, eyes open, and
listened to the moans of his men and the dripping
of water somewhere in the back of the cave.

He cursed himself for a fool. He should have
tried to fight. He should have tried to run. He
should have done *something*, even if the goblins
killed him on the spot. Anything would have been
better than being chained up in this confinement.

He shifted a bit, and the heavy iron shackles on
his feet made a muted clanging sound. He could
have wept in despair. Captured by goblins . . . it

was a human's worst nightmare. He pressed his eyes shut and felt tears trickle from their corners.

After chaining them so they could barely move, the goblins had carried them down to a lower level of caves and locked them in a dark cell. Water dripped slowly in the back. Escape seemed ever farther away.

And, over the last few hours, the goblins had returned periodically. "Good eating!" they said each time, as they hauled a man out. Then Bowspear would hear a brief struggle in the corridor outside, followed by a human scream and the thud of a falling body. Afterward would come a faint jingle of shackles . . . a dead body being dragged away.

He'd shuddered. Now there were only three of them left in here. He heard skittering goblin footsteps outside the cell and saw the flicker of torchlight under the door. Slowly he scrambled backward, deeper into the darkness.

The door swung open and a goblin stepped in . . . followed by a human. Bowspear stared up at the stranger in polished chain mail, with his deepset eyes, short black beard, and sharp prominent nose.

"Get up," the man said.

Slowly Bowspear climbed to his feet. The others did the same.

The man held out his hand. From it dangled the Eye of Vadakkar. Bowspear's breath caught in his throat.

"Which one of you wore this?" the stranger demanded.

"I did," Bowspear said. It came out as little more than a croak.

The man took a torch from one of the goblins and thrust it closer to Bowspear's face, looking him over carefully.

"You don't look like a wizard," he said.

"I'm not," he said. "I am Captain Parniel Bowspear of Grabentod."

"How do you explain *this*, Captain Bowspear?" He held up the Eye again.

Bowspear remained silent. Perhaps, if he could make this man *think* he was a wizard . . .

"I thought so," the man said. He nodded to the goblin. "You did well. You will be rewarded."

After tucking the Eye of Vadakkar into his pocket, he grabbed Bowspear's chain and pulled him toward the door.

"Come," he said. "My mistress wishes a few words with you."

Bowspear dragged his feet. "My men—" he began.

The stranger hauled him into the rough stone passageway. More goblins were waiting there, and they all held long knives. As soon as the stranger had dragged Bowspear out of the way, they poured into the cell.

"I'm afraid," the stranger said, "they're lunch."

Screams echoed from the cell. Goblins began to gnash their teeth happily, and a small river of deep red blood washed out the open cell door and down the passage.

Bowspear gulped, feeling sick.

* * * * *

Harrach dreamed of beautiful women flying toward him with arms outstretched. He reached out to embrace them, but something kept blowing them away, like rose petals caught on the wind. When finally he did manage to touch the hand of one, it felt cold and damp, like a corpse's.

He came awake suddenly, very afraid, though he didn't know why. His heart pounded wildly; a cold sweat covered him. For a second he didn't know where he was, but then it all came back. In the Hag's Domain . . . surely that alone was enough to cause nightmares.

He blinked. The campfire had almost gone out, he realized with alarm. Silent as a cat, he rolled from his blanket and drew his sword. Who was supposed to be on watch? He hesitated, glancing around anxiously. It felt early, certainly no later than midnight.

Softly, he moved around the camp, counting sleeping bodies. One too few. Everyone was present except Captain Evann . . . and Evann had taken the first watch.

He moved to Lothar's side and shook him awake.

"Wha—" Lothar asked, blinking sleepily.

"Shh!" he whispered. "Something's wrong! The captain's gone!"

Instantly Lothar snapped awake. "What happened?" he asked in a low voice.

"I don't know. I'm going to investigate . . . I'll

take Uwe. Stand watch. If we don't come back, wake the rest of the men and retreat to the forest. Got it?"

"Aye, sir," he said.

Harrach gave a quick nod, then crossed to Uwe and gently shook him awake. As soon as Harrach told him what had happened, the lad leapt to his feet and eagerly drew his sword. He even puffed out his chest, doubtless proud to have been chosen for such a dangerous assignment, and Harrach didn't have the heart to tell him the truth: Uwe was the most expendable of all the men here. That alone made him Harrach's first choice.

Turning, Harrach padded cautiously from the ruined building, with Uwe on his heels. He saw no trace of Captain Evann anywhere, nor any signs of who might have taken him. If only it were light, he thought with a frown, he'd be able to look for tracks in the grass.

At the edge of the ruined village, he paused, listening over the low moan of the wind. He heard the susurrous hiss of wind blowing through the grass, the soft lapping of waves from the lake, but other than that . . . nothing. He shivered, a little unsettled. Out here he would have expected at least a few distant cries from owls hunting mice by moonlight, but no living creatures stirred.

Uwe lightly touched his arm. Harrach glanced over impatiently. What was it?

Slowly, Uwe pointed toward the lake. Harrach followed the line of his finger to a pair of figures on the shore . . . a man and a woman? Could one of them be Captain Evann? Squinting, Harrach tried to see, but in the dimness he couldn't quite tell.

"Come on," he said, advancing for the lake cautiously. He had no intention of being taken by surprise—the waist-high grass could have hidden an entire army.

The figures on the shore turned and began walking away from them. They seemed to be walking on top of the water, heading toward the center of the lake. For a second, Harrach thought they had to be walking on ice, but then he saw the waves around them, under their feet.

Then, like an early morning mist, they vanished.

"Ghosts!" he breathed.

Uwe looked at him, bewildered. "That wasn't the captain?" he asked. "What happened to him?

"Yes, it was Captain Evann," Harrach said with a shudder, knowing somehow that it had been his friend and commander. "He's beyond our help, though."

* * * * *

Captain Evann felt himself drawn to this strange pale woman. Her kiss, long and lingering, left him hungry for more. He reached for her, but she shook her head and drew back.

"Who are you?" he whispered. "Why do I love you so?"

"This way, Terrill . . ."

Taking him by the hand, she led him to the lake.

He went willingly. Every time she looked at him, his heart fluttered in his chest like a dove's wings. He wanted nothing more than to be with her for the rest of his life. He found himself gazing at her face, admiring her delicate nose, the soft curve of her cheek. . . .

Taking his hand, she led him away from the village, down to the shore of the lake. There, without hesitation, she stepped onto the water and began walking away from the shore. He hesitated a moment, afraid of losing her, afraid of being left behind. The farther she got from him, the more desperate he became. Finally, unable to stand the thought of losing her, he ran after her.

Instead of splashing into the chill water, though, he found himself gliding like a ghost on top of it, but the movement seemed like the most natural thing in the world. He was amazed he'd never done it before. Catching up with her, he took her hand again, and she did not pull away. A deep contentedness filled him.

At last they came to a small, mist-shrouded island in the center of the lake. Here, the woman released his hand.

In a second she vanished, leaving him alone. He blinked and suddenly felt himself released from her spell. What had happened? Why had he gone with her? Had she been real?

Slowly he wandered forward, looking all around, and only then did he notice the bones. The whole island was covered in them . . . the pale weathered gray remains of many people. He swallowed as he picked up an arm bone, turning it to the moonlight. He noticed deep cut marks, the kind made by a sword, gouged into it. This person had been cut down in a battle of some kind.

He crossed the narrow rocky island, following the trail of skeletons. There had to be dozens of them, perhaps hundreds, but it must have happened many years ago for them to be this weathered.

"Terrill . . ." a soft voice whispered.

He turned. The woman had reappeared, but this time she didn't touch him, didn't do anything except float before him, her feet suspended half a foot from the ground.

"Who are you?" he demanded.

Her voice was soft and hollow. "I am one of the people from the village where you camped."

"But you're . . ."

"A ghost," she whispered. "Yes, Terrill . . ."

"What do you want?" he asked. "Why have you brought me here? To kill me?"

"We are forgotten here," she said. "Behold—"

A blinding light surrounded him. Evann covered his eyes, crying out in surprise.

—And suddenly he heard battle cries and screams from women and children.

Opening his eyes, he gaped at the scene before him.

It had suddenly become daylight. He stood in the middle of the village as it must have looked many years ago. All the houses stood whole, their thatched roofs and brightly painted shutters in repair. The warm breeze ruffling his hair and beard tasted of summer, and he felt the hot sun on his back, smelled fresh-mown hay from the fields around the town—

Hooves thundered. He whirled to see a dozen horsemen in dark helms riding with swords drawn through the village. Women and children ran before them, screaming in terror. Here and there a few men stood, holding pitchforks and axes, trying in vain to drive them off.

Evann shuddered as he saw one, then another, and another of the villagers fall. The horsemen were cutting them all down, men and women and children alike. The warriors moved with mechanical speed, killing and killing and killing until the streets ran with blood—

"Enough!" he cried, covering his eyes. It was too terrible to watch.

Abruptly he stood on the island in the middle of the lake. The ghost floated before him.

"So . . ." she said.

Evann gave a shudder and met her eyes. "Who were they? The Hag's minions?"

"Who?" she asked.

"The Hag—" he began, then stopped. They had probably never even heard of her. Their first encounter with her minions must have been their last.

"She is an abomination," he said. "She rules this land now."

"It must have been her," the ghost said.

"What do you want of me?"

"Peace," she whispered. "The quiet, easy sleep of those who rest in their graves. . . ."

Harrach nodded. "That I would promise you," he said, "but I have no way to get my men to this island. It's been years since anyone lived here. There are no boats left anywhere on shore."

"If you cannot come to us, we must come to you."

Evann felt a strange stirring of energies, and around him the bones began to move. Body after body began to reassemble itself, bone crawling to bone, hand to arm to shoulder . . . foot to leg to pelvis . . . ribs—backbones—skulls—

One by one, the skeletons rose up before him—tens, then dozens of them, men and women and children. Empty eye sockets gaped at him; flesh-less bones rattled as they moved.

Evann swallowed. This was magic, but somehow it felt good, like an age-old wound being closed. Slowly, the skeletons turned to face the shore, and then they began to walk out across the waves.

The ghostly woman took his hand and pulled him after them. Hardly daring to believe, Evann stepped out onto the water and followed.

* * * * *

Harrach saw them coming across the water.

"No . . ." he breathed. It had to be an undead army. He'd heard the Hag sometimes controlled creatures from the Shadow World, but he'd never believed he would encounter them here. The encampment in the village must have attracted the Hag's attention.

"Back!" he whispered to Uwe. "Rally the others. Tell them to ready their weapons outside the house."

"But the captain—"

"Do it!"

"Sir!" Uwe ran.

Swallowing, Harrach drew his long sword. He'd stand point guard, then fall back as they approached. Harrach spotted Captain Evann, following after the skeletons, holding the hand of a beautiful, pale woman. He and his escort were walking a few inches above the waves.

"Magic!" he breathed. Evann looked alive and well, but that might be a trick of some kind.

Hesitating, Harrach considered what their best course would be. They could fall back, retreating to the forest, but that might be what the Hag wanted. On the other hand, if they stood here, they might be able to rescue Captain Evann.

As the skeletons set foot ashore, they began lying down on the sand. Harrach glanced to the east. The sun had just begun to pale the sky with the morning twilight . . . perhaps they marched only in darkness.

Captain Evann set foot ashore just as the sun broke over the mountains to the east, flooding the land with light. He stood there, looking around him as if half bewildered. A trap? Harrach hesitated, then cautiously advanced.

"Captain?" he called. "Is that you?"

"Aye," Evann said wearily.

"What happened?"

"We have to bury them," he said. "I promised."

* * * * *

Bowspear allowed himself to be dragged through the mountain and out a small cave on the other side into daylit forest. There, the mail-armored man released his leg shackles so he could walk. He found it hard to care anymore, though. His men were dead. *Eaten.* A numb shock filled him.

The man half led, half dragged him down through a small pass to a grassy plain, where a squad of ten men waited with horses. They all wore helms with the insignia of Drachenward on the front . . . though the markings had been all but obliterated by scratches.

Rapidly, the men saddled the horses. They had an extra one, which they led over to him.

"Get on," said the man who had dragged him.

The horses . . . the Drachenward helms . . . suddenly it all made sense to Bowspear. He almost laughed with relief.

"You're Orin Hawk, aren't you?" he asked.

"Yes." Hawk's voice was low.

Perhaps everything wasn't lost after all, Bowspear realized. Perhaps sacrificing his men wasn't such a great cost.

Licking his lips, he began, "I need to talk to you—"

Hawk whirled and struck him backhanded across the mouth. "Shut up. Get on your horse. You'll talk plenty before the day is through."

Stung by the blow, Bowspear did as Hawk commanded. Once Bowspear was in the saddle, Hawk turned and, without a word, mounted his own horse, spurred it on, and rode to the head of the line of men.

They rode for perhaps two hours, skirting the mountains, until they reached a small camp. Bowspear noticed with growing unease that not one of the soldiers around him spoke during the entire trip. There seemed to be little human about them except their forms.

Their camp, nestled between two low hills, consisted of a dozen tents, several long, low buildings, and a few pens that held more horses. A large natural cave opened up in one of the hills.

Hawk rode up to the cave and dismounted. "Mistress!" he called. "I have him for you."

Seconds later, Bowspear saw movement in the shadows.

A hideous creature emerged—a hideous pockmarked woman from the waist up, a mass of huge, writhing serpents from the waist down. An unreasoning terror like none he had ever felt before filled him. He wanted to run screaming from her camp and never return.

Hawk chuckled, a low, evil sound. Bowspear managed to tear his gaze from the Hag long enough to look at the man.

"Beautiful, isn't she?" he said, awe in his voice.

He really felt that way, Bowspear realized. He swallowed. She had bewitched him.

The Hag made a gentle clucking sound deep in her throat. Bowspear faced her and tried to keep his fear and revulsion from showing. Perhaps all was not yet lost. He'd found Hawk, after all. If she'd make a deal with him . . .

"Well, pretty-pretty," she said. "So you thought you could fool me, did you?" She gave a cackle and stretched out her hand to stroke his cheek.

Bowspear couldn't help himself—he recoiled in revulsion.

"Take him inside," the Hag said to Hawk, and then she retreated into the cave, vanishing in the deep shadows.

"Yes, Mistress," he said.

Hawk dragged Bowspear from the saddle, then marched him into the cave. Bowspear tried to keep from vomiting. The place had a thick foul odor, like something had died in here and begun to rot.

"Have mercy!" he gasped, trying to breathe.

"Mercy? What's that?" Hawk hooked Bowspear's manacles to a steel chain. It ran through a thick iron ring hammered into the cave's ceiling, then over to a hook set into the far wall.

Slowly, drawing the process out, Hawk began to pull the chain tight. They were going to torture him, Bowspear realized suddenly. He began to struggle, trying to slip his arms free of the manacles. He could barely breathe, barely think. Panic filled him, and he began to flail his limbs like a drowning man.

Hawk gave the chain a long jerk, and Bowspear felt his arms fly up over his head. Hawk gave a second jerk, this time hauling Bowspear upward. He dangled by his wrists six inches off the floor. The heavy iron manacles bit into his wrists, and blood began to trickle down his arms.

"Her pleasure," Hawk said with a smile, "is almost always fatal."

* * * * *

Harlmut quickly assembled twenty of his guards, then personally led them into the city in search of the assassin. It had been many years since he'd been to the Temple of Ela, but he remembered the way well enough. With quick gestures, he sent half his men to one side of the building and half to the other, surrounding the temple. Only when they signaled their readiness did he step forward.

"Come out, Haltengabben!" he cried.

Instantly, she appeared through the front doors. She'd been watching them, he realized. If their actions concerned her, she did not show it. Her features remained smooth, calm, impassive.

"What is the problem, Harlmut?" she asked in a soft voice.

"An assassin tried to kill one of my guests in the market this morning," he said. She would have no way of knowing how much he knew, so he might as well go for everything. "Witnesses spotted him fleeing here. You will surrender him to me now."

"An assassin! Here?" She shook her head, looking bewildered. Harlmut wasn't surprised—of course she would deny it. "Surely you are mistaken."

"Do you have any visitors staying here?" he demanded. "Anyone new to Grabentod?"

"Well . . ." She hesitated. "There is one man visiting us, though I haven't met him yet. If you'd like to interview him, I see no harm in that. I am certain he's not the assassin you're looking for. He's a trader from Grevesmühl, and he's offering rare spices that we use in some of the temple ceremonies."

Harlmut motioned to four of his men. "Get this trader," he said. "Bring him out to me. But take caution—if he's the assassin, he may prove dangerous."

"Aye, sir," they said.

Haltengabben turned to lead the four soldiers inside. When they disappeared from view, Harlmut began to pace, a trifle nervous. He had a feeling he wouldn't like whatever they found.

A few minutes later, one of the guards returned, wearing a disgusted look on his face.

"He's dead, sir," he reported to Harlmut. "Killed, it looks, by his own hand."

Sighing inwardly, Harlmut accompanied him into the temple, through the entry hall, into the altar room, then into back rooms. He should have expected something like this. Haltengabben knew enough to cover her tracks.

He found her standing in the doorway to a small guest chamber, shaking her head as though in disbelief.

"I cannot believe it," she said softly to Harlmut. "Suicide in the temple . . . it's unheard of."

He brushed past her.

The assassin had hanged himself with a rope. The man's black tongue protruded from his mouth, and his eyes bulged hugely in their sockets. On the desk sat a pair of knives.

Harlmut picked one of them up and held the blade to the light. A greasy gray liquid covered the blade . . . it had been coated with something, some poison. Mari had been right.

"Cut him down," he said to his men. "Take the body outside the city and burn it."

"Such a shame . . ." Haltengabben said.

"It's suicide, then," he said, looking at her.

She met his gaze unflinchingly. "So it would seem."

"I trust you won't allow this sort of visitor in the Temple of Ela again."

"Of course not," she said. "I have no idea how he could have gotten in here. His credentials must have been forged."

"Of course." Harlmut stared at her until she shifted uncomfortably. "Come to the castle this evening," he said firmly. "I think it's time we spoke. I'll have dinner prepared for just the two of us."

"Very well," she said. "I am honored, Harlmut."

* * * * *

After Harlmut left, Haltengabben stormed into her office and slammed the door. She felt like hurting someone. Very carefully, she controlled her rage.

He'd cost her a very expensive assassin. She'd have to make reparations to the Grevesmühl branch of the Temple of Ela to compensate for their loss.

He'd been sloppy. He'd almost been caught, and he'd led them to her. If he'd talked . . . she didn't take chances. She'd had to kill him.

Dinner tonight . . . she could imagine what Harlmut wanted. Her support never came cheaply. But with Bowspear gone, it couldn't hurt to listen to what he had to say.

ANUIRE

eighteen

Bowspear's arms ached. He shifted, trying to relieve the pain in his wrists and shoulders, but the movement made things only worse. Groaning, he tried to catch his breath.

He'd been left hanging here for what felt like hours. Several times the pain had grown so intense that he'd blacked out.

Now, he opened his eyes to find the Hag standing before him. The masses of serpents that made up the lower half of her body writhed and undulated and hissed. He moaned in pain and fear.

"Pretty-pretty, what lovely skin you have," the Hag said, reaching out and caressing his cheek again.

He tried to pull away, but she seized his head with both hands and stared deeply into his eyes. Bowspear felt a cold shock run through him. He began to tremble all over.

Slowly she brought her face close to his, and then she licked him very gently on the tip of his nose.

He shuddered. "What do you want?" he whispered.

"The truth, pretty-pretty." She released him. Slowly he began to turn on the chain before her. She showed him the Eye of Vadakkar. "What brings you through the goblin mountains armed with a trinket such as this?"

"I came to kill Orin Hawk," he said.

She cackled as if this were the funniest thing she had ever heard. "Kill my pretty boy? Why?"

He hesitated. Perhaps he could bargain with her. The information had to be worth something to her, perhaps even his life.

"Release me, and I'll tell you," he said, trying to sound bold.

"I have a better idea," she said, catching him and looking into his eyes. Her pupils seemed to grow larger, peering into his soul. "You will tell me everything, because you love me."

"I . . . love . . . you . . ." he felt himself whispering.

He blinked, and suddenly it was true. He realized he loved her more deeply than he had ever loved anything or anyone in his life. Her face . . . her hair . . . her eyes . . . even the serpents that made up the lower half of her body . . . He had never seen anyone more gorgeous. He loved her. He wanted her for his own.

He tried to reach for her and found his arms caught in chains. Struggling against them only made him spin more quickly. Why didn't she let him down? Couldn't she see how he loved her? He longed to rush to her, to hug her to him, to possess her and never let her go.

"There, there, my pretty," she crooned. Softly she stroked his hair. "Tell me all you know, and I'll release you."

Quickly, eagerly, he told her everything: about the wizard who'd come to Grabentod, about Harlmut's mad plans to save Orin Hawk and bargain for the release of King Graben.

Then he told her how he longed to rule Grabentod himself. "I'll make you my queen when I have the throne," he promised. He could see it all in his mind, "We'll rule together—"

"All you would-be princelings say that," she said wryly. "I could be a queen twenty times over, if promises came true!"

Rising, she headed for the mouth of her cave.

"Wait!" Bowspear called after her. "Release me! I love you! *I love you*—"

"If promises came true . . ." She gave another cackle, then was gone.

Bowspear began to weep.

* * * * *

Candabraxis woke in pain. His whole body seemed to be on fire. He struggled to sit up.

"Lie back!" an old woman's voice said.

He tried to focus on her. "I must—"

"You must sleep." She pressed what felt like a cup to his lips, and he found himself gulping a sweet-smelling broth of some kind.

Almost at once he felt himself drifting away. Everything had a fuzzy look.

"Sleep," the old woman said again. "Sleep . . ."

* * * * *

Harlmut had an elegant table set for two that evening in one of Castle Graben's smaller dining rooms. He stood in the doorway, surveying the fine Anuirean bone china, the gold forks, spoons, knives, goblets, and finger bowls, the intricate lace tablecloth and napkins. Yes, he thought, this would certainly do for entertaining Haltengabben. It was more than she deserved.

At seven o'clock, the high priestess arrived with a small retinue. Harlmut met her and ran through all the tedious formalities, then escorted Haltengabben in to their meal.

"Your people can eat in the kitchens," he told her. If she noticed the implied insult, she made no sign of it.

"This is the first time you've invited me to dine with you," she commented as he seated her at one end of the long table. "I had begun to think you might be avoiding me, Harlmut."

"Not at all," he said. "I am not the king, and I have no desire to rule Grabentod. Necessity has forced this position on me. I hold no more banquets or celebrations than the court demands, and I entertain no one myself . . . until now, that is."

She raised her elegantly plucked eyebrows slightly. "Ah? And why do I deserve such an honor?"

He took a chilled bottle of Anuirean summer wine and filled her crystal goblet. "Why do you think?" he asked.

"Perhaps . . . to eliminate one you mistakenly perceive as a rival for the throne?"

She smelled the wine, tasted it gently with her tongue, then set it down. Harlmut frowned a little. Did she think him a common poisoner? If he had wanted her dead, it could have been accomplished far more quickly and far more subtly. She wasn't the only one, after all, with connections to assassins. King Graben had several times removed troublesome relatives and ambitious captains like Bowspear, and Harlmut had acted as go-between on each occasion.

"I wish to strengthen the ties between the Temple of Ela and the king," Harlmut said firmly. "I fear they may have become . . . shall we say, *frayed?*"

"How so?"

"May I speak openly?"

"It would be a pleasant change," she admitted.

"The world is overfull of subterfuge in these troubled days."

Harlmut leaned on the table. "I know you and Bowspear have conspired to seize the throne," he said.

Quickly Haltengabben murmured her denial.

"No, let me finish," he went on. "I also know that Bowspear has gone to prevent Captain Evann from retrieving Orin Hawk from his accursed servitude to the Hag. And I know that you equipped him with certain, ah, *magical* protections to help him in this task."

The last was a guess, but from the way Haltengabben's eyes widened in surprise, he knew he'd hit upon the truth. This time she did not bother to deny it.

"I can understand your feelings in this matter," he went on with a dismissive gesture. "King Graben is far away, and surely it must appear his grasp on Grabentod is slipping away. On the other hand, Parniel Bowspear is here, and his men would follow him to the Shadow World itself—aye, most of Grabentod would if he asked. Indeed, he is successful in everything he tries."

"True." Haltengabben nodded almost imperceptibly.

"However," Harlmut said, "the right to rule Alber is in the blood, not the sword. Bowspear is popular, but he comes from common birth. He can never rule Grabentod. It's unthinkable."

"Stranger things have happened," Haltengabben said softly.

She must be thinking of Ulrich Graben, Harlmut realized.

She smiled. "And yet I have a strange feeling your hold here is stronger than you realize, Harlmut. The people do not fear you . . . but they like you, and they love their king. As long as you rule in his name, and you rule fairly and well, I think you will find you have more supporters than you know."

"About the wizard . . ."

"I did not order his death," she said firmly.

A little to his surprise, Harlmut found he believed her. Even so, he suspected she hadn't told him everything. And if she hadn't ordered Candabraxis's murder, then who did? How was the Temple of Ela involved?

Perhaps it had been the Hag. Everything seemed to revolve around her. He knew she had ties running deep into Grabentod. . . .

Haltengabben rose suddenly. "I thank you for a most interesting meal," she said amiably. "I hope we will be able to have another such meeting soon, Regent."

That was the first time she'd ever called him that, Harlmut realized with a sudden flash of pride. He rose and nodded politely to her as she swept from the room. Perhaps the meal had not been a waste of time after all.

* * * * *

Captain Evann and his men worked throughout

the morning, cutting frozen turf with their swords, then scooping dirt from the holes to make a series of shallow graves.

There were forty-seven skeletons. Each had to be laid out neatly, arms carefully folded, every bone in place. Then Evann murmured a prayer for the soul of the dead man, woman, or child, and his men began to bury the bones.

It was hard work, but at last it was done. Wiping sweat from his brow, Evann sat, staring out across the water to the small isle. For some reason the Hag's minions had dumped all the bodies there. Why? He shook his head. It was a puzzle he might never unravel.

His men joined him, panting, sweaty, dirty. At least the weather had begun to warm up some, he thought. It was well above freezing now.

Rising, he went down to the lake and washed the dirt from his hands and face. The others did the same, sputtering and shivering when the cold water hit them.

Drying his hands on his pants, Evann looked to the north. The Hag's main camp would be somewhere that direction, he thought. They still had a long distance to go today.

He returned to the encampment, picked up his pack, shrugged it on, and called, "Let's get moving!"

They struck out across the plain, following game trails. Here and there rose small clumps of trees, islands in an ocean of grass.

Suddenly Evann spotted movement far ahead

of them—horses, he thought.

"Down!" Harrach hissed.

Everyone dropped to the ground. Evann raised himself up on his knees to peer ahead.

There were thirty or forty horsemen, all heading in their direction at a gallop. He swallowed. Had they been seen?

"Quickly," he said, turning to his men, "keep low and follow me."

Crouching, Evann ran for the nearest cluster of trees, perhaps a hundred fifty yards away. They might be able to hide there, or at least make a stand to defend themselves.

The company didn't quite reach the trees, though. The pounding of hooves neared, and suddenly the horsemen were circling them.

Drawing his sword, Evann stood. "Form a ring!" he shouted, and his men did so, facing outward, weapons ready.

The leader of the horsemen reigned in. He was a tall man with a dark beard, a large prominent nose, and intense eyes.

"Who are you?" he demanded. "Why do you trespass on the Hag's Domain?"

Evann stepped forward. "I seek a man known as Orin Hawk," he proclaimed.

"What do you want with him?"

"I have a message for him and him alone."

"Then you've found me," the man said. "What is this message?"

"I need you to return with me to Grabentod."

"I fought your people before finding my true

destiny here. Why should I return to the home-land of my former enemies?"

Evann paused. He didn't quite know what to say. He had not expected to so quickly run upon the man, and had no speeches prepared. "Be-cause," he finally said, "you and only you can bring peace to our land. And, for that matter, peace between Grabentod and Drachenward."

Hawk laughed bitterly. "Lay down your arms," he said, "and your lives will be spared . . . for now."

"You must know what she's done to you," Evann pressed. He looked from Hawk to each of Hawk's men. "You're under her spell—you're *all* under her spell. Don't you want to be free? Don't you want to be men again? Come back with me and—"

Hawk threw back his head and laughed. "Take them!" he cried. Then he spurred his horse toward Evann, raising his sword.

ANUIRE

nineteen

Evann barely had time to raise his sword in defense. He parried Hawk's savage blow; the force of it jarred him all the way to his shoulder. Evann countered.

Laughing in savage glee, Hawk smashed his blow aside and tried to ride him down.

Rolling, Evann barely managed to avoid being trampled. He came up on his knees, caught his balance, and dodged before Hawk could wheel and charge him again.

Things were not going well. Each of Evann's

men held off two or three fighters; Harrach parried four. Several men suddenly cried out in pain—but whether they were his or Hawk's, Evann couldn't say.

Still laughing, Hawk swung from the saddle and advanced on foot. "This is too easy," he said. "You can do better, can't you? I'm not even working up a sweat."

Grim faced, Evann retreated before him. At least he had only one man to battle, he thought. If he could manage to disarm Hawk and force him to surrender—

Hawk rushed him suddenly. Parrying, feinting, parrying again, trying to keep that blur of steel from finding his body, Evann retreated before the savage onslaught. It couldn't go on much longer, he knew. All he had to do was play for time and let Hawk exhaust himself. If only he could make it to the trees, he thought, he might stand a better chance there—

Suddenly he stumbled over something on the ground behind him. Arms windmilling, he fell backward, landing on his elbows. He'd fallen over Uwe's body, he realized with dismay, though he couldn't tell whether the lad still lived.

With a laugh, Hawk gripped his long sword in both hands, set his feet, and gave a huge powerful swing. The force of it knocked Evann's sword flying. Evann searched frantically for Uwe's weapon, but couldn't find it anywhere.

Hawk stepped forward and placed the tip of his sword to Evann's throat.

"Yield," he said, serious at last. "No more of your men have to die here."

"I yield," Evann said softly.

"Hold, men!" Hawk shouted. "They yield!"

Gradually the sounds of combat ceased. Evann looked around and found only four of his men still standing. He swallowed. A pitiful end to their adventure, indeed, he thought.

Hawk stepped back and offered Evann his hand. Slowly, without accepting it, Evann climbed to his feet. His right arm felt numb from the blow that had knocked his sword away. A sick heaviness filled his chest and stomach.

"Lay down your swords," he said to his men. He could barely speak. "We surrender."

Lesser men might have wept. Evann forced himself stiffly upright. At least, as he'd once heard King Graben say, while you lived, you still had hope.

As he watched, first Lothar, then Harrach, then the others lowered their weapons. Hawk's men moved forward, disarming everyone. Only Harrach had done real damage; two men lay dead at his feet.

And Uwe—Evann knelt to check on the boy. He was breathing, but unconscious from a blow to the head. Blood covered the right side of his face. He also had a deep cut on his right arm and another on his side, laying bare his ribs.

Evann looked up. "Is there a healer among your men?" he asked Hawk.

"He'll be sewn up at camp. If he lives that long."

Evann swallowed. They'd been fools to believe they could sweep in here and kidnap Hawk. Bowspear had to be laughing at them now, calling them fools and toasting their deaths.

He glanced at the others. Reddman and Shurdan were on their feet again, nursing arm wounds. They wouldn't be fighting again in a long time, he thought. They were down to four swordsmen. The odds did not look good.

"Line up." Hawk commanded, returning to his horse and swinging up into the saddle. "It's a long march back to camp, but we can make it by nightfall if you run."

Evann slowly rose. "We'll need a litter."

Hawk motioned to two of his men, and they galloped to the small patch of trees. Evann watched them dismount, take hand axes from their saddlebags, and begin hacking down saplings.

* * * * *

Evann had become completely disoriented and had no idea where they were. A long rope tied his wrists to Hawk's saddle, and he stumbled a bit as he allowed himself to be pulled along. He didn't have the strength to struggle anymore—not that it would have done any good, guarded as he and his men were by so many of Hawk's soldiers. They had been half marched and half dragged across the plain all the day. Now, in darkness, they had reached a new chain of mountains.

Rounding a low hill, they came upon a large

camp of several dozen tents and a few long, low wooden buildings. Several huge bonfires burned, and tall torches had been stuck into the ground, providing light.

The tents formed a semicircle around the mouth of a cave. Hawk drew up there and dismounted.

Panting, bone weary, Evann sank to the ground. Around him, his men did the same. He felt sick and dizzy. His arms ached. Cuts and bruises covered his knees and legs, mementos from all the times he'd fallen and been dragged.

Hawk had shown no compassion or mercy. He had called only two short breaks, and neither Evann nor his men had been given any water. Perhaps Uwe had been the lucky one, he thought, despairing.

Hawk swung down from his saddle and handed the reins to one of his men. The others began leading the horses off toward one of the long, low buildings . . . probably stables, Evann thought.

Hawk didn't seem to think the prisoners were very dangerous anymore. Exhausted, with their hands tied, sprawled on the cold, hard ground, Evann knew they wouldn't be a match for anyone.

Hawk grinned cruelly as he gazed down at Evann. "Not so full of spirit now, are you?"

Evann closed his eyes and winced. He wished he'd fought to the death.

Laughing, Hawk stepped to the mouth of the cave. A faint sickly green glow seeped from somewhere deep within.

"My lady!" Hawk called, stepping into the cave.

"We met with success!"

"You have them, pretty-pretty?" asked a high warbling voice like fingernails on slate. Evann shuddered at the sound.

"Yes, my lady!" Hawk vanished from sight. Evann thought he heard sounds of kissing from within.

An instant later Hawk returned, a broad grin on his face. Taking Evann's rope, Hawk jerked him to his feet.

"Your prisoners," he called into the cave, "are waiting, my lady!"

Evann saw movement in the shadows. Slowly a creature—a hideous old woman from the waist up, a mass of huge serpents from the waist down—glided forward slowly and into the torchlight.

Evann felt his heart seize up. He wanted to go screaming into the night. He wanted to run and never look back. How could they have hoped to succeed against this *thing*?

"Magic!" the Hag hissed, drawing to a stop before them. She reached out and ripped the protective talisman from Evann's cloak, then went down the row of prisoners, doing the same to each of Evann's men. She threw each of Candabraxis's little protective charms to the ground, spitting on them and letting her serpentine abdomen writhe upon them, grinding them into the earth.

"What do you have to say?" she demanded of Evann when she finished. "You invaded my lands. You brought foul magics before me. Why should I not kill you? It would be a simple thing, my pretty-pretty one."

Evann shuddered and averted his gaze. "We mean you no harm," he said, trying to keep his voice from cracking in fear.

Hawk said, "They claimed to be searching for me. They want me to return with them and end some battle in Grabentod."

"Fools . . ." the Hag said.

"What do you want me to do with them?" Hawk asked. "Shall I string them up, so you can watch their bodies twisting in the wind?"

She cackled. "Such pretty-pretties they would be! No, no, sweet boy, I will attend to them myself, one by one, boiling them to make powerful potions." She produced an inhumanly shrill laugh.

Evann felt a chill run down his back. It was a fate he wouldn't have wished on even Parniel Bowspear.

"As you will, Mistress," Hawk said with a grin.

Still cackling, the Hag undulated toward her cave and vanished from sight.

Hawk turned to go, but Evann leapt forward to block his way. They wouldn't have much time before the Hag called them. There had to be some way Evann could save his men.

Then he saw the talismans lying on the ground where the Hag had thrown them. They seemed a little muddy, but unhurt. If they were still potent—

"Hawk," he said, "I know now where your loyalties lie. The Hag is a powerful mistress. But I beg you, at least have mercy on the boy. He's done you no harm."

"Eh?" Hawk turned to look at Uwe. He frowned a little, as if remembering his own youth.

Evann pressed his point. "The Hag would never miss such a little one. I can make it worth your while to save him."

"How?"

"I'll pay you—you're a soldier. You know the value of gold."

"You have gold?" Hawk asked. He looked Evann over slowly. "Where? My men didn't find any when they searched you."

"It's hidden," he said. "It's inside my amulet—yes, there on the ground." He nodded toward the spot where the talismans lay.

Hawk bent and picked one off the ground. A subtle change swept over his face as he held it in his hands, turning it over and over. His expression lost some of its sharpness, and the ruthless, fanatical gleam in his eye seemed to fade.

Or had Evann imagined it? He hesitated, unsure. What if Hawk had another charm? Would two double their power? He had to try it.

He licked his lips. "I don't think it's that one," he said quickly. "The one lying next to it . . . yes, there."

Hawk picked up a second talisman. As he held them both in his hands, he turned to Evann, and it seemed to Evann that a strangely confused look crossed his face.

"What—" he whispered.

"Yes," Evann breathed. The amulets were working. Together, two of them had begun to protect Hawk from the Hag's charm.

"Get a third one!" he said.

Hawk slowly turned toward the cave. "Mistress . . ." he whispered.

"She's nothing to you," Evann said in a low voice. "You don't need her. She's bewitched you. What you need are more of the amulets. There's gold hidden in all of them. *Pick them up*, Hawk. Pick them *all* up."

Numbly, like a mindless puppet, Hawk obeyed. Evann watched as he gathered up one, then another, then another. When he held the last of them, he froze, staring at Evann and the others as if aware of them for the first time.

"You—" he said, confused. "I think—we—"

"Quickly!" Evann said. "Pin the amulets onto your cloak. They'll protect you."

Hawk obeyed, fingers fumbling.

"We must escape before the Hag returns," Evann went on softly. "Give me your knife. I'll cut my men free. Then we'll all escape together."

"Escape." Hawk glanced sidelong at the Hag's cave for a moment, then drew his knife and stepped forward. In one quick movement he severed the ropes around Evann's wrists.

Fingers half numb from cold and loss of circulation from the ropes, Evann massaged his wrists for a second. Then, gently, he pried the blade from Hawk's grasp.

Harrach had seen what was happening and

crawled closer, arms outstretched. Evann slit his ropes, too, then passed him the knife.

"Cut everyone else free," he said.

"Aye, sir." Harrach rubbed the feeling back into his hands. "Do we run?"

Evann hesitated. "No. Stay here, in line, on the ground, like there's nothing wrong. We don't want to arouse suspicion yet."

"Aye, sir," Harrach said. He turned and started sawing at Lothar's bonds.

Standing, Evann grabbed Hawk by the elbow and propelled him toward the stables. He felt a sudden rush of energy now that he had a plan. They'd need mounts next.

"When we get inside, order ten horses saddled," he told Hawk.

"Horses . . ." Hawk mumbled.

He seemed dazed, hardly able to think. It had to be the result of the Hag's magic wearing off after years of being enslaved to her.

"Snap to, soldier! You have your orders!"

"Yes, sir!" Hawk straightened and seemed to draw on inner reserves of strength.

Evann held his breath. He'd given Hawk strong orders hoping his training and instincts would take over—but would it work?

Side by side, they ducked through a low doorway into the stables. Evann surveyed the long rows of stalls, each one occupied. The air inside smelled thick from horses, hay, and manure.

One of Hawk's men had been rubbing down a gray mare. Hawk strode up to him without hesitation. "Saddle ten horses," he said to the soldier on duty. "Have them waiting for me in twenty minutes."

"Sir?" The soldier looked from Hawk to Evann and back again. He was one of the men who'd helped Hawk capture them, Evann thought. If he suspected something . . .

Hawk snapped, "You heard me, Hrell. Ten horses. I have a mission tonight."

"Yes, sir!" The man hurried to obey.

Evann whispered, "Our swords next."

Turning, Hawk strode out into the camp again. Without hesitation, he headed for one of the smaller tents.

Evann trailed him. It was working, he thought, scarcely able to believe his fortune. His hands were trembling. They were going to make it. If only the Hag stayed in her cave until they could get away. . . .

Hawk swept back the tent flap. Inside stood racks of swords, several pikes, crossbows, and other weapons. Clearly they'd found the camp's armory. All their weapons had been piled just inside. Evann pulled his sword from the heap and belted it on, then retrieved his two knives. Meanwhile Hawk gathered up the other weapons taken from Evann's men.

As he worked, Evann studied Hawk. The man seemed strangely withdrawn.

"I loved her," Hawk said slowly. "Do you know that, Evann? I loved her."

Evann didn't know what to say. "You'll be home

soon," he promised. "Your family loves you, too."

They ducked out of the tent. Evann looked over the camp briefly. His own men still sat or sprawled or lay before the Hag's cave as if prisoners. All of Hawk's men had gone into the larger tents. The horses, he assumed, would be waiting for them in the stables. Everything seemed to be going right for once.

"Get your men ready," Hawk said to him. "I'll bring the horses."

"You're sure . . . ?" Evann said softly.

Hawk gave a nod. "Yes. Now hurry, before the Hag returns."

ANUIRE

TWENTY

The Hag sat in her cave staring deep into her cauldron. As she watched, Captain Evann scurried around her camp like a chicken with its head cut off, dragging the creature he thought was Orin Hawk to the stables, then to the armory tent, then back to his men. She chuckled. If he only knew the truth, it would frighten him as much as she had.

The serpents where her feet should have been led out a series of hissing sighs. They sensed her triumphant mood.

"What do you think, pretty-pretty?" she asked.

Beside her, the real Orin Hawk shifted. He was staring down at the cauldron as well, watching the scene outside.

"Will it work?" he asked. "Will that creature fool them?"

"Don't my plans always work?"

"Yes," he said. He kissed the back of her neck. She smiled.

"*Yesssss* . . ." she echoed. She began to scream with laughter.

* * * * *

Candabraxis woke suddenly from a light fever. He sat up, not sure where he was.

"Light!" he commanded in a croaking voice. A glowing sphere of energy sprang into existence overhead. Its wan glow showed him his bed-chamber in Castle Graben's east tower.

Suddenly everything came back to him. The market—the man who'd tried to stab him—

"Easy," said a woman's soft voice. "Lie back, now."

He focused on her: an old woman with a plain face, graying brown hair, and clear blue eyes. She had a shawl around her shoulders. She'd been sitting up beside him.

"Who are you?" he said. "What happened to me?"

"My name is Mari," she said. "You were nearly killed in the market." She told him all that had happened and how she had saved his life.

"I am indebted to you," he said softly. He sank back, staring up at the ceiling.

"You are indebted to no one," Mari said. "It is our duty to strive against the dark forces whenever they appear among us."

"You know magic?" he asked. He propped himself up on his elbows and regarded her with new interest. His master had talked like that at times. Duty, responsibility, fighting for justice—these things had been stressed to him time and again throughout his studies. He'd thought these lessons merely the eccentricities of an old wizard, but now . . .

"No," she said, "I know no magic. I am just a poor old healer. But I listen and I learn. My grandmother, now, *she* had a real talent, bless her."

"I think you sell your skills too cheaply, Mari. But perhaps that's best, if you want to avoid notice by the dark forces."

She smiled. "Perhaps." Taking up her knitting, she began work again. It was another shawl, this one yellow and peach.

He looked off to the distance, considering all that had happened. Good and evil had seemed like such abstract concepts in his studies. Now that he'd encountered the dark forces, now that they had almost killed him, he felt as though a veil had been lifted from his eyes. No longer academic concepts, they had become all too real.

It had to have been the Hag, he thought. Somehow she'd become aware of him. Her attempts to scry on him told him that much. Perhaps his flash-of-light spell had done more than drive her away. Perhaps it had angered her enough to make her want to kill him.

But *why?* He had never done anything to her. Or had he?

With a sick feeling in his stomach, he recalled suggesting the rescue of Orin Hawk. Had that been enough for her to have him murdered?

He pressed his eyes shut. *Probably.* One who attracts the attention of an abomination as powerful as the Hag has to expect things like this to happen.

Duty. Responsibility. Justice.

He understood now. It all came clear. He had been drawn to Grabentod not for some great personal destiny, but to learn the nature of life.

I have to fight for what I believe in, he told himself. I have to make a difference in the world.

Clearly the Hag feared his powers. Why else would she try to kill him at such a distance and at such a great effort? And for such a being as her to fear him, he must pose a threat to her, or at least to her comfort and security.

He sat upright, taking a series of deep breaths. For a second his head swam drunkenly, but then the universe steadied around him. Bandages swathed his right hand, and when he wiggled his fingers experimentally, a sharp stab of pain traveled from his palm to his elbow.

"You must rest!" Mari protested.

"I have too much to do," he said with determination.

A thousand ideas surged through his mind—spells and counterspells, charms and elixirs and potions. And then he conceived of something new—a huge, powerful rune of protection like none he'd ever seen before. It hung in his mind, a vision of perfection.

He could do it, he knew suddenly. He could protect Castle Graben from the Hag.

* * * * *

The serpent reared back, looking Haltengabben in the eyes. Its fangs glistened with poison. Its tongue flicked out, tasting the air.

Haltengabben concealed her shudder of disgust and fear by picking up the small silver knife on her desk. She used it for a letter opener, but it could be a deadly weapon in her hands as well.

"Ssssooo," the serpent said, "what of our bargain?"

"I have taken steps—"

"The wizard is still alive!"

"The wizard is under the protection of the regent," Haltengabben said. "Things are difficult. I need more time to work—"

"No more time!" The serpent wove its head before her and gave a low hiss. "The contract is canceled! I will dispose of the wizard myself!"

Rearing back, the serpent faded from view, evaporating like a morning fog beneath a hot sun.

Haltengabben swallowed. She almost felt sorry for the wizard. *Almost.*

Mostly she felt sorry for herself. A pound of gold, lost . . . and now she'd have to make up for the assassin's death from her own pocket.

ANUIRE

twenty-one

The journey back to Grabentod was nothing short of a nightmare.

Hawk led them up into the mountains behind the Hag's camp and through a small pass that would have been treacherous by daylight. By night, it was almost impassable. The horses stumbled and skidded on crumbling shale, patches of ice, and loose rocks. Only by dismounting and plodding at a snail's pace did they finally reach another high wide cave. At Hawk's request, the men mounted again, and headed toward the cave mouth. This cavern had torches burning inside, and Evann glimpsed dozens of goblin warriors lining the walls.

"Pay them no heed," Hawk said. "The Hag has a truce with them. We may pass at will through their territory, as they may pass through ours."

Swallowing nervously, Evann obeyed. He saw how his men clung tight to their reins, gazes fastened on the rough stone floor ahead of them.

And so they rode through the heart of the mountain, passing close enough to a goblin city to hear the ringing of a blacksmith's hammer, hideous croaking voices raised in song, and sounds of axes clanging against axes—military drills or sport of some kind, he supposed.

From time to time Evann stole quick glances up side tunnels, and each time he glimpsed small groups of goblins watching them from the shadows. They wore steel helms with horns on top and mismatched plate armor, and carried wicked looking axes in their gnarled, bony hands.

Hawk might have free passage through here, Evann realized, but he had no friends. These goblins would just as soon have killed them all.

Toward morning, they emerged from a smaller cave, one just large enough for their horses to slip through. It was dawn outside, and the sudden sunlight and sharply colder air brought Evann up short.

They'd been riding all night. Now, he realized, looking at the mountains around them, they'd emerged close to the southeastern corner of

Grabentod. *Home!* He could have cried with relief.

Drawing a deep breath, Evann led his men forward. Suddenly he wanted to get as far from the goblin caves as possible. The Hag had doubtless already missed Hawk . . . and if she sent the goblins after them, he knew they wouldn't stand much chance.

"I've been here before," Hawk said, riding up next to him as their horses picked their way down the slope toward the foothills below.

"Oh?" Evann glanced over at him. Hawk looked drained, with huge dark circles under his eyes and new, deep-etched lines around his mouth and forehead. The Hag's magic had taken its toll on him, Evann thought grimly.

Hawk nodded. "We used to hunt here. There's an abandoned farmstead ahead, just beyond that hill. We can rest safely there."

Evann glanced back. "The goblins, though . . . surely we need more distance to be safe."

"They won't venture into Grabentod," Hawk said firmly. "I don't know why . . . but they won't. The Hag tried to get them to attack your lands for years, but they always refused."

"Ah." Evann considered that bit of information. If they were safe here, then they should make camp. He felt worn to his bones, and his men looked exhausted, almost ready to drop.

Evann nodded. "Lead the way," he said to Hawk. "We'll spend the day here."

Hawk spurred his horse, and its plodding steps quickened a little, following a narrow trail down.

Half an hour later they reached the abandoned farm. The main building consisted of crumbling stone walls, none more than four feet high, surrounded by high scrub brush and a scattering of twisted pine trees. It had a barren, desolate feel, as though nobody had been here in many years.

Evann dismounted, surveying the scene. It would do, he thought, once they had a fire going. Here there would be no ghosts to bother them.

Quickly giving the orders, he helped Hawk drag Uwe's litter into the ruins. The boy did not look good. His eyes were deeply sunken, his cheekbones were swollen, and his skin looked more like clay than flesh and blood.

"I'll tend to him," Hawk said. "I have some knowledge of healing. See to your men and camp."

"You're sure?" Evann asked.

Hawk nodded briefly. "I'll do all that's needed."

It took an hour to set camp properly. At last, with two sentries posted, a large fire in the middle of the ruins, and the horses fed and tethered and under warm blankets, Captain Evann returned to Hawk's side.

"How is he?" he asked.

"Not good," Hawk said grimly. "The trip through the mountain was too much for him, I fear."

Uwe suddenly stirred and moaned. A little color had come back into his cheeks.

"He looks a little better," Evann ventured.

"It's the fever. It's put color back in his cheeks.

We'll keep him close to the fire today and hope it breaks. . . . He may live to see another day, but I would not count on it."

Evann nodded grimly. Of all his men, Uwe might have been the most expendable . . . but in many ways he had been Captain Evann's favorite. Evann had seen a lot of himself in Uwe, and he'd hoped to raise him right.

"We'll pray for the best," he said.

* * * * *

Over Mari's protests, Candabraxis rose and went into his workroom. She followed him.

"You must rest!"

"I don't have time," he said. "There is too much to do . . . there is too much I have to accomplish!"

He gathered up an armload of jars and set out for the stairs. At the doorway a sudden pang stabbed him in the stomach, and he gasped in pain. Two of the jars fell free, smashing on the floor and scattering dry powders everywhere.

"I told you!" Mari said, grabbing his arm and pulling him back toward his bed. "You can get up tomorrow, if you feel up to it. Not a moment sooner!"

"But—"

She shook her head firmly. "Not another word. I'll call the guards and have you restrained—if I have to!"

Candabraxis took a shuddering breath as another pain stabbed him. This time he managed to hang on to his jars, though.

"Maybe I'd better," he muttered. There would always be plenty of time tomorrow. . . .

* * * * *

Evann spent most of the day helping Harrach hunt for meat, and together they brought down a stag. The camp had roast venison for dinner.

Warm and yawning, his belly full, Evann sent his men to bed and walked first sentry duty himself. The cold, clear night seemed to hold promise. Uwe, somehow, still managed to cling to life. They had rescued Hawk. There was no apparent pursuit from the Hag or the goblins. He nodded. Everything had turned out well enough. Now, if they could only get their king back . . .

Around midnight, he awakened Harrach for sentry duty and then turned in. Evann fell into a deep sleep almost instantly.

Then, suddenly, he awoke with the certainty that something had gone wrong. He didn't know what told him aside from an unmistakable feeling deep inside.

The fire burned low, providing a dim flickering orange light. He listened, but heard nothing out of the ordinary, just the soft snores of the men around him. Reddman paced outside the farmhouse on sentry. It was nearly dawn.

Rising, Evann padded softly around the camp. Everyone was present. Kneeling beside Uwe, he touched the boy's forehead to check his fever—then recoiled in shock.

The boy's flesh was cold as ice. . . . Uwe was dead.

That had to be what had awakened him. He felt a deep wrenching inside, as though a part of himself had been torn away. Another friend lost on this mission. It had better prove worth the expense. King Graben had better be freed.

"What is it?" Hawk asked, sitting up suddenly beside Uwe.

"He's dead."

Hawk threw off his blanket and checked Uwe, too. Then he sat back and shook his head. "There wasn't anything we could do for him," he said softly. "I sat up with him part of the night, holding his hand when I heard him cry out in his sleep. At least he felt no pain. This was a better death than the Hag would have given him."

"We'll bury him at first light," Evann said, voice suddenly husky. "Then . . ."

He found he couldn't continue. Rising, he went out to walk alone, away from camp, and wait for the sunrise.

"I'm sorry, lad," he whispered, half to himself. "I'm so sorry."

* * * * *

They spent the morning hours cutting a grave in the frozen earth for Uwe. They laid his body out properly, as a warrior deserved—with hands folded across his chest, the hilt of his sword between them. Then they covered the grave with loose rocks. It was hardly the funeral cairn the boy deserved, Evann thought, but it was the best they could do so far from home.

"He was a friend and a comrade who died too young," Harrach said. "The gods will look after him."

That seemed like a fitting close. Taking a deep breath, Evann tried to put the events of the morning behind him. He had lost many men over the years, friends and relatives both, but seldom had their deaths hit him as hard as Uwe's. It seemed so *needless.*

"Let's go," he said gruffly, turning toward camp. "We have a long distance to go today."

"Forty miles on horseback is easy enough," Hawk said eagerly. "We can be in Alber tonight."

Evann glanced at him a trifle angrily. "We just buried a friend. We'll get to Grabentod in good time."

"Of course," Hawk murmured. "That was thoughtless of me. I'm sorry . . . years trapped in the Hag's service have cost me my manners, I'm afraid."

"It's nothing," Evann said. He made a dismissive gesture with one hand.

Even so, Evann wondered . . . Death is a universal among soldiers, and a soldier shows respect at a companion's funeral even if he wasn't a friend. It is one of those things everyone does. To a man of the sword, it is as much an instinct as breathing.

Eagerness to return to civilization after years with the Hag, though . . . he could see how that might make Hawk want to rush. He might have felt the same way himself after being so long from home.

* * * * *

The next day, around noon, Candabraxis awoke. In his mind, he still saw the spell that he wanted to create to protect Castle Graben. It was a massive rune, surrounding and incorporating all of the castle walls and towers and buildings, a rune so large and powerful that not even the Hag herself would be able to penetrate it.

Rising, he found Mari asleep in a chair by the door. Good, he thought, it will make work much easier without her interfering. He felt stronger today. He knew he could make it outside without her help.

He went into his workroom. First things first: his hand. The wound felt sore today, a dull constant ache, but not at all as sharp.

He rolled up his right sleeve, unfastened the bandage, and carefully began to peel it back. Blood had stiffened the cloth, but fortunately it wasn't stuck to the wound.

Wincing, he saw the long jagged cut, carefully closed with a seamstress's tiny, meticulous stitches. It had already begun to heal . . . and it would be quite a scar, a long white line running from the tip of his thumb to the heel of his palm. Slowly he flexed all his fingers. Yes, he thought, he could work with only a little discomfort.

He found a clean bandage and redressed his wound, adding a few lotions from his own stores to speed the healing process.

Then, changing into clean gray robes, he began gathering up the tools he would need. Mari, he found, had swept up the herbs he had dropped yesterday and put them in new jars. He smiled. She was a good woman, had worked hard, and deserved to sleep.

He, on the other hand, had work to do. . . .

* * * * *

Parniel Bowspear hung, suspended by his arms, shivering and half naked, from a hook in the ceiling of the Hag's cave. His hands and wrists ached, and sharp pains shot through his shoulders. His tongue felt thick and fuzzy; breath came in quick rasps. He prayed he'd die soon.

A cackling laugh broke into his thoughts. Raising his head slightly, he gazed down at the Hag through swollen, bloodshot eyes.

"Kill me and be done with it," he tried to say. All that came out, though, was a low, gasping moan.

"What say you, my pretty-pretty?" the Hag asked in mockery. "You want down?"

"Kill . . . me.!" He felt a brief triumph that those words had come out clearly.

"Very well, pretty-pretty."

The Hag crossed to the wall and released the rope tied there. It snaked up, through the ring in the ceiling, and Bowspear fell to the floor with it.

He couldn't move his arms. He whimpered. He'd never felt so much pain in his life.

"Oh, you'll scream," the Hag said, advancing on him, the serpents attached to her lower body hissing in delight. "I'll have my pleasure first . . . and if you satisfy me, you'll live."

With the strength of twenty crones, she picked him up, and as she kissed him, her dank breath foul as the stink of a swamp, her serpents twining around his body in a crushing embrace.

Bowspear began to scream.

ANUIRE

TWENTY-TWO

Candabraxis worked at a feverish pitch throughout the morning. He began in the castle's kitchens, coopting every spare child he could find . . . twenty-two in all, ranging in age from perhaps eight to thirteen or fourteen.

"This is a great magic," he told them when he had gathered them all in the central courtyard. The other servants—their mothers and fathers, mostly—had seemed all too eager to get them out from underfoot. "When it is done, all of Alber will be protected from the Hag. But, to accomplish it, I will need your help."

They looked at each other, shifting uncomfortably in the cold breeze. "How?" one of the older boys called. "What can we do? We know nothing of magic."

"Ah!" Candabraxis said. "An excellent question. It shows you have a good mind, boy. How can you help? By keeping people away from the rune I will draw until I am finished with it!"

He jogged to his tower and picked up two of the jars he had set there earlier. Inside both were a mixture of peldane root and hog's blood, which he would use to mark out the rune. Dipping a brush into the mixture, he began painting a huge line across the courtyard. This would be the nexus for the rune, the line that held it all together. As long as it was complete, no other wizard's magic would be able to penetrate it, not even the Hag's. This was the vision that had come to him in his fevered sleep.

"Watch and learn," he breathed, speaking half to himself and half to the Hag. "Watch and fear the true power of a wizard!"

He began the second line, then the third, then a long sweeping arc that would extend all the way around the castle, incorporating its outer walls into the huge magical pattern.

* * * * *

In late afternoon, Evann rounded a grove of trees and came within sight of Alber. The city, set on the low hills, still lay an hour's ride away, but the captain and his companions would sleep inside tonight.

He had pushed them hard to reach the city. The horses, exhausted, had begun to lag. Now everyone pulled up around him.

"Ride ahead and let Harlmut know we've returned, and successfully," he said to Harrach. "Nothing must happen to our guest until King Graben is freed."

"Aye, sir," Harrach said. He spurred his horse and galloped ahead.

"So that is Alber," Hawk said. "It's smaller than I thought it would be."

"Small, but fierce as a cornered wolf," Evann said. "We can more than take care of ourselves, Hawk. And remember who rescued you . . . something your own people never managed."

He smiled thinly. "Of course. Come, it's nearing dinnertime. I wish to meet this regent of yours. And I'd love a cup of hot mulled ale. . . ."

* * * * *

It was finally done.

From the roof of his tower, Candabraxis surveyed the rune he had drawn around and through Castle Graben. He was awed. He wondered again at the forces that had driven him to create it. It was as though divine inspiration had guided his hand through the process.

Slowly he turned, following the graceful sweep

of every line, the intricate way in which the outer walls worked themselves into the total pattern, becoming an integral part of the rune.

Only one step remained: casting the actual spell that would energize the rune and make Castle Graben safe for the first time since he had arrived. It was the last part, and the smallest, but hardly the easiest.

Spreading his arms and closing his eyes, Candabraxis summoned the powers within himself. This was the difference between a truly great wizard and a novice. With enough schooling and the right teacher, anyone could learn rudimentary control over the forces of magic. A true wizard, though, could reach down to the core of his being, then beyond, into the primal force of the world itself, the wellspring from which all true magic flowed. He had read a hundred different books that described the process. Some said it resembled the turning of a key. Others compared it to breaking through a dam and letting the onrushing flood sweep the mage before it, all the while steering it toward his goal.

Candabraxis found it like none of those. He envisioned a river of light running through the world. With his sheer force of will, he could change its course, ripping it from its bed and turning it loose in any direction he chose, to any task he needed done. He felt it pouring through him now, tingling in his veins and arteries, coursing through his heart.

"Now!" he cried.

The light burst forth from him, channeling into

the rune, creating a barrier that not even the Hag would be able to penetrate.

And just as quickly, it was done.

He sagged back, drained, exhausted. It had worked, the greatest magic of his life, and it had worked. He felt exhilarated. *It had worked!*

* * * * *

Harlmut visited the Temple of Ela that night.

Haltengabben came out to see him at once. "Regent," she said, sounding surprised, "what brings you here at this hour?"

"I need someone to send a message to Drachenward," he said bluntly.

"And you want me to go?" she laughed. "How odd."

"I know you have ways of getting messages to other temples," Harlmut said, "and this one you may find of interest, since it affects you, too."

"How so?"

"Captain Evann rescued Orin Hawk from the Hag's clutches. They're both in the castle."

"How . . . daring of him. And what of Bowspear?"

He shrugged. "Missing . . . gone . . . and good riddance!"

She chuckled. "It seems your plans have worked admirably. You have a prisoner—"

"Guest, rather," Harlmut said quickly. No sense using such provocative language if it could be avoided.

"Guest, then. And your only rival has mysteriously vanished. Why, if I were of a more suspicious nature, I might think you had done away with him."

Harlmut snorted. She was baiting him.

He said, "We will return Hawk to Drachenward. We would like to invite an ambassador from their king to visit us to verify the truth of our claims. In return, we want Drachenward to intercede on King Graben's behalf with the merchants of Müden. It is, I think, a reasonable request, given the immense favor we have done them in rescuing Hawk."

Haltengabben inclined her head. "Very well. And I would like to meet this Orin Hawk."

"I'm sure that can be arranged," Harlmut said, "*after* the ambassador has arrived."

* * * * *

Guard duty at Castle Graben offered a life of tedious repetition, exactly as Mikkan wanted.

This late in life, he enjoyed the pleasures of routine, knowing exactly what he had to do each day, exactly when to do it, and exactly how much it paid. At sixty-two, he no longer felt the urge to fight and wallow in blood and conquest. He'd had enough of that in his boisterous youth at sea as a raider, and still more of it in his long but undistinguished career as an officer, which had ended in a second mate's berth. The year he'd lost two fingers off his left hand to a heavily armed Müden ship, he decided to retire from the sea. He could still hold a sword, aye, but he couldn't do any of the shipboard tasks even an officer needed to be able to perform. So he had settled into semi-retirement as a castle guard. And why not? It paid well enough, gave him a post deserving of respect, and allowed him to keep serving the king.

His duties normally took him completely through the castle three times a night. First, he circled the high outer walls on the ramparts, noting that the four sentries on duty were all awake and alert, then went down and around the inner courtyards, then inside the castle itself.

As always, everything seemed unremarkable. As always, not a tapestry, not a table, not a chair was out of place. Mikkan sighed with contentment. Yes, he liked his life as a guard.

He rounded a corner and came face-to-face with a man. It was that stranger, Orin Hawk, whom Captain Evann had brought back. What was he doing out of his room, in this part of the castle, at this hour? It had to be treachery of some kind. Never trust a Drachenwarder, that's what his pa always used to say.

"Here now," he began, drawing his sword. "What are you doing here?"

In reply, Hawk leapt forward, one hand closing around Mikkan's throat, forcing him back against the wall with a thump. Choking, trying to wrench himself free, Mikkan dropped his sword and grabbed Hawk's hand.

Skin and flesh sloughed off under his fingers

like overcooked meat from a bone. Horrified, strangling, Mikkan gazed in horror at the bare bones of a skeletal arm now strangling him. Hawk tightened his grip. Mikkan felt as though his lungs would burst. He had to draw a breath. He had to free himself somehow.

His only hope lay in the knife at his belt. His vision was already growing dark around the edges. He didn't have much time left.

His fumbling fingers found the knife's hilt. Drawing it, he plunged it deep into Hawk's belly, working the blade up and into the man's chest, aiming for the heart. With satisfaction, Mikkan felt the blade slide across bones. That should do it, he thought, trying to push free with the last of his strength.

"You can't kill me that way," Hawk said, grinning down at him. "I'm already dead, you see."

That grinning death mask was the last think Mikkan saw before darkness took him.

ANUIRE

Twenty-Three

"Is it plague?" Harlmut asked softly.

That was just what they needed now—an outbreak of disease to kill Hawk and ruin their chance of freeing King Graben. The scullery maids who'd found old Mikkan's body had fled the kitchens shrieking in terror. It reminded him of his childhood, when the Gray Death had swept through Grabentod, killing one of every three adults and two of every three children. He shuddered.

"No," Mari said shortly. She and Candabraxis continued to examine the old guard's body, now stretched out on a table in Candabraxis's workroom.

"Then what?" he prompted.

"His blood is gone," Candabraxis said, stepping back and wiping his hands on a clean white cloth. He met Harlmut's gaze. "But that didn't kill him."

"Aye," Mari said. "He was strangled, sure enough. See these bruise marks on his neck, Regent?"

Harlmut peered at them, then frowned. "Strangled, then his blood removed? How can that be? And why?"

"Magic," Mari breathed. She glanced at Candabraxis, who nodded curtly.

"There's no wound on the body to show such blood loss," the wizard said. "If I didn't know better, I would say the Hag has begun her revenge."

"The Hag . . ." Harlmut felt his fear turn to anger. "Perhaps I should have expected retribution for stealing Hawk from her."

Candabraxis shook his head. "But there must be another explanation. Yesterday I drew a protective rune around the castle. The magic worked perfectly. It should protect us from outside sorcery. None of the Hag's minions would be able to pass through the castle gates."

"Then how do you explain this?" Harlmut indicated the body.

"I don't know," Candabraxis said, frowning. "I must study the matter."

"Do so," Harlmut said. "Plague or magical attack . . . this cannot be allowed to happen again."

* * * * *

Later, in the royal audience hall, Harlmut discussed details of the Hag's camp with Captain Evann and Orin Hawk. A runner burst into the chamber.

Instantly, Harlmut leapt to his feet. "What's wrong?" he demanded.

"Sir!" Gasping, the man drew up before him. "A ship—from Drachenward—coming now—"

Harlmut nodded. "I believe," he said to Hawk, "an ambassador has arrived from your people. Captain Evann, if you'd be so good as to meet him at the docks?"

"Aye, sir," Evann said with a grin. "That I will."

* * * * *

His Eminence, Duke Leor of Drachenward, waddled slowly down the gangplank as though he owned Grabentod. That was the only way to enter an enemy state—with all due ceremony. He had little expectation of success here. Nobody in Drachenward's court believed the mad claim that Grabentod had rescued Orin Hawk from the Hag. After all, Drachenward's army had been trying for years without success.

Fifteen men-at-arms followed behind him. All wore dress uniforms, but Leor knew their true mission was to protect him. If this were some ruse designed to trap or kill him, they would make Grabentod pay dearly for it.

Leor's chest gleamed silver and gold with his fifteen medals for military prowess. He had won them forty years ago, in his youth, in various campaigns against goblins, orogs, and neighboring states. At age forty, after his retirement to life in court, he had steadily gained both weight and influence. Now, weighing four hundred pounds, he had the king's undivided attention. In fact, the king had personally dispatched him to lay these absurd claims to rest.

Leor's black boots shone with a mirrorlike polish. Every bit of his uniform, from the imperial red pants and shirt to the gold epaulets on his shoulders and the high red-plumed helm, had been neatly pressed, creased, or brushed to optimum effect.

His steady gaze took in the small group of untidy men who had assembled to greet him on the dock. Rabble, all of them. He strode forward, looking to the one in front—a large, barrel-chested man with a short black beard and piercing gray eyes. That had to be their leader, he thought.

"I am Duke Leor," he announced with a slight bow.

"Pleased to meet you, sir," the man said with a leering grin. "I am Captain Terrill Evann, one of the king's men."

"You aren't the regent?" Leor demanded. Somehow it wasn't surprising that they didn't know proper diplomatic protocol.

"No," Evann said. "Regent Harlmut asked me to meet you and escort you to Castle Graben. Rooms are being prepared for your stay."

Leor glanced around. No coaches or carriages

seemed in evidence. Did they expect him to walk through the streets like a commoner? Well, so be it—the sooner he got it over with, the sooner he could get home. Already he hated this little kingdom of pirates.

"Very well," he said, keeping his tone carefully noncommittal. No sense antagonizing them. If they didn't know what they were doing, he would use that to his advantage later. "Please, lead the way, sir."

Without a word, Evann turned and began to hike toward the castle above. Leor's honor guard fell in around them.

Fifteen minutes later, puffing and near exhaustion, soaked in sweat despite the cold, Leor reached the castle gates. His heart hammered wildly in his chest, and he thought he'd be sick. He struggled to keep his composure. He wasn't as young as he used to be. He should have asked for a coach. They would have provided one if he'd insisted. It would have been far more dignified than arriving huffing and blotchy-faced.

Evann escorted him to the audience hall, a dingy little room less than a third as large as he'd expected. A thin, pinch-faced man sat on the low throne, waiting for him. Four guards stood in attendance.

"We are pleased to welcome you to Grabentod," the man said formally. "I bid you welcome to our land in the name of King Graben."

"On behalf of Drachenward, I accept your welcome," Leor said, studying the regent. Here, at least, was a man who knew some manners. "I am Duke Leor."

Harlmut inclined his head slightly. "I am Harlmut, regent for King Graben." He rose. "Please, let us retire for a more informal meeting. We have refreshments waiting."

"Ah?" It defied protocol, but Leor wanted a drink very badly right now, and a chair would have been doubly welcome. "Of course," he murmured. He motioned for two of his men to accompany him.

Harlmut showed them into a smaller room just off the audience chamber. A fire burned cheerfully in the fireplace, and bright tapestries hung on the walls. He took all this in through the briefest of glances, because his eyes had fastened on the table in the center of the room.

There, spread out in a delightful series of artfully arranged platters, were delicacies he normally enjoyed only on the highest holidays in Drachenward. Anuirean summer wines and sweetmeats . . . truffles from Grevesmühl . . . oatcakes soaked in syrup from Aerenwe . . . and a dozen more such treats. He finally selected a small spiced cake and bit into it. Softer than any he'd tasted before, sweet as honey, with a strawberry paste at its center, it sent him into paroxysms of delight.

Perhaps, he allowed, these provincials from Grabentod were not as uncivilized as he'd feared. Seating himself at the table, he poured a goblet full of wine and sipped gently. He had no fear of poison; they would not have brought him all this way to poison him so quickly, not with so many of his guards present.

"Delectable," he announced, smacking his lips. "An excellent year, served at the perfect temperature."

Harlmut poured himself a goblet of wine and sipped.

"You say you've rescued one of our men from the Hag," Leor said.

"True," Harlmut said. "And we did it at great expense and loss of life, may I add."

"But *why*, I wonder?" Leor said.

"We want our king back."

"Müden has him, not Drachenward."

"Also true. But Drachenward is not without influence."

Leor made a deprecating gesture. "I think you overestimate our importance in Müden's internal affairs."

"And there is the matter of Hawk's lineage."

Leor's brow furrowed. Lineage? What did that have to do with anything? Orin Hawk's father, Oluvar, had been the sixth-born to the old king, but that hardly mattered since Oluvar's eldest brother had ascended the throne. That placed Hawk far from Drachenward's throne. Twenty men had better claims than he.

Then he remembered Hawk's mother. She had come from Müden, he recalled . . . from the powerful Erbrecht family. Harlmut's plan came clear to him then. It was Orin Hawk's connection to the

Erbrechts that would free King Graben, not his connection to the Drachenward throne.

"Yes," he breathed. "I see what you mean." He looked around. "However, I see no proof of Orin Hawk's rescue. What say you to this?"

Harlmut rang a small bell on the table. A door in the back of the room opened, and a slender man with a short black beard and pronounced features stepped out. His gaze found Leor, and an instant later, he grinned happily.

"Your Eminence!" Hawk said.

"Baron Hawk," Leor said, rising. Although it had been years since he'd last seen Orin Hawk, Leor recognized him instantly. There could be no mistake.

He spread his arms, and Hawk gave him a brief embrace, slapping him on the back.

"I hardly recognized you," Hawk said. "You've changed a good deal since I last saw you, Leor."

The duke patted his belly. "Success agrees with me."

Harlmut cleared his throat. "If I may . . ." he said.

"Of course." Leor took the opportunity to seat himself again, taking another strawberry-filled cake.

"I-ll wait outside, Eminence," Hawk said. "I know I'm in good hands with you." Nodding politely to Harlmut, he went back out the way he'd come.

"He looks well," Leor said to Harlmut. He leaned back, looking at the regent with new respect. The man who could rescue Orin Hawk from the Hag had to be a formidable opponent, indeed, he thought. Perhaps it would soon be time to broach the subject of a new peace with Graben-tod. . . .

"Yes," Harlmut said. "We are happy to have rendered this small service to Drachenward."

"Bring me writing implements," Leor said. "I must compose a letter to my king about this situation."

Harlmut opened a drawer in the table and pulled out parchment, quill pen, inkwell, and sealing wax. Leor knew exactly what he wanted to say. Despite the barbarity of the land, they had done the near-impossible and freed Hawk. In regard to that service, he felt it their natural duty and obligation to intercede with the Erbrechts on King Graben's behalf. . . .

* * * * *

That night, Harlmut held another celebration for the court—this one in honor of Duke Leor and his entourage. Arriving fashionably late, Candabraxis found his normal seat to Harlmut's right occupied by the duke. That suited him fine. Harlmut, he had found, possessed a knack for getting people to talk about themselves, and he wanted to know more about their guests.

As he slipped into his chair, the castle musicians struck up a lively tune, the one to which he'd taught Lady Delma the Grevesmühl Waltz. She rose at once and curtsied to Duke Leor.

"Your Eminence," she said, fanning herself coyly, "I would be honored if you would escort me to the dance floor."

Leor laughed. "I'm too old for dancing," he said. "I leave that to younger men. Dance with young Hawk here," he said, clapping Hawk on the shoulder.

"I would be honored," Hawk said, rising. He circled the table and offered his arm, and she took it.

Candabraxis watched them sweep into the waltz. Lady Delma was whispering instructions to Hawk, and though his steps were a little more halting and awkward than Candabraxis would have expected from a nobleman, he seemed to please Lady Delma. Other dancers joined them on the floor until it seemed half the court was there.

"Your people do enjoy themselves in their king's absence," Leor observed a little dryly.

"Surely that's human nature," Candabraxis said.

Leor looked at him as if noticing his presence for the first time. "And you are . . . ?" he asked bluntly.

"Ythril Candabraxis." He smiled most charmingly.

"Our wizard," Harlmut added.

Leor leaned back in his seat and regarded him with more interest. "Ah, I should have smelled magic in young Hawk's rescue."

"My contributions were inconsequential," Candabraxis said. "The true hero is Captain Evann, who almost single-handedly fought his way through goblin-infested mountains, defeating many minions of the Hag, until he found Hawk and rescued him. But I'm sure you've heard that story enough times today."

"Yes," Leor said. He glanced back to Harlmut. "Tell me more of your plans. Have you considered the advantages of a real peace with Drachenward, instead of our present unfriendly truce?"

"I must admit I've long thought such an alliance would be mutually beneficial," Harlmut said, "but such things must wait until King Graben returns. I am, after all, merely his regent. However, with your help, we should have him back by spring."

"Indeed," Leor said, "as long as the weather holds, I don't see why he couldn't be back here before the end of winter."

Candabraxis smiled with satisfaction. His plan had worked admirably well. No one, not every Bowspear, would be able to stop King Graben's return now.

Briefly, he wondered what had happened to Bowspear. If he were dead, there truly would be nothing left to interfere with Harlmut's rule until the king's return. Perhaps, Candabraxis thought, he should try to scry on him again. After this many days, and this much battle, Bowspear's protective charm might have gotten separated from him.

Yes, Candabraxis decided, he'd try scrying on him again tonight.

ANUIRE

twenty-four

Full of food and slightly drunk, Candabraxis returned to his room. No sense scrying on Bowspear now, he thought. He wanted sleep. Tomorrow would be soon enough.

He opened the door to his suite and went into his sitting room. The castle's servants had banked his fire for the night, and though his rooms felt a little chilly, they didn't have that icy edge he hated. He shrugged off his heavy cloak and hung it on a peg by the door.

Bed now, he thought, yawning.

He headed into his bedroom. As he did, a dark shape suddenly loomed out at him from the shadows.

Instantly awake, he leapt back. An assassin? Had one of the Hag's creatures somehow made it through his protections?

It was only Orin Hawk, though. Candabraxis relaxed a little. What would bring Hawk here, to his private rooms?

"Did you want something?" the mage asked a little suspiciously. "I generally like people to wait for me in my sitting room."

"Yes," Hawk said, advancing steadily.

"What?"

Candabraxis continued to retreat. Something was wrong. There was a strangely hungry look in Hawk's eye, almost a bloodlust. The wizard swallowed uneasily. A spell of petrification, he thought, would do the trick . . . something to stop Hawk without hurting him.

He began the spell as he backed into the wall. Still Hawk continued his advance. Candabraxis slid to the left, heading for the doorway.

Finishing the spell, he launched it at Hawk.

Instantly Hawk froze.

Relaxing, Candabraxis took a deep breath. What had gotten into the Drachenwarder? Why had he come here?

Puzzled, he circled Hawk slowly, then stepped forward to look at the man's eyes more closely. There was something strange about them. . . .

As soon as he was within a foot of Hawk,

though, the man's right hand shot out and grabbed him around the throat. Candabraxis, choking, pounded at Hawk's arm, trying to free himself. The Drachenwarder's grip was unnaturally strong.

Hawk's eyes had begun to glow faintly red. He wasn't human, Candabraxis realized. It was a trick of the Hag's.

"Fool," the creature posing as Orin Hawk hissed, tightening its grip. "You can't stop the undead with spells designed for mortals."

Candabraxis found his vision darkening, and he began to panic. His lungs ached. He felt like his throat was going to cave in. He flailed wildly, striking the creature in the face again and again, but with no effect. He had to breathe—

No! an inner voice cried. *Discipline!*

That was what his old master said would save him from any problem.

Patience.

Discipline.

Reason and thought.

The creature had to be undead. Clearly it had killed the guard last night, taking his blood. So how could it get past his protective rune?

With a charm . . . the same sort of charm he'd used to send Evann and the others into the Hag's Domain. That had to be the answer.

With his last effort, Candabraxis forced his eyes down, beyond the arm of the creature, searching its clothing for anything that it might use to protect itself.

Suddenly his eye fastened on a talisman just poking out from under its cloak. It looked familiar—

He grabbed for it with the last of his strength. His fingers closed around it, and he ripped it away and threw it across the room in one sudden motion.

The creature howled in pain and released him. Spinning backward, it collapsed and began to writhe on the floor. The full force of the castle's protective magic had struck it.

Gasping, choking, Candabraxis sucked in air like a drowning man. A wave of dizziness and nausea hit, and he had to catch himself against the wall to keep from falling.

Barely conscious, he watched the illusion surrounding the creature roll back. Its skin turned green and greasy; bits of bone showed through tears in its flesh. Its eyes, glowing with a sickly red light, slowly went dim.

As it lay there, it began to smolder, and suddenly tongues of clear blue flame flickered over its body, consuming it. Two minutes later, only an ashen gray smudge marked the spot where it had fallen.

Candabraxis staggered into his workroom and fell into a chair. His throat ached; he could barely breathe or swallow. But he was alive. That was all that mattered.

He'd been lucky, he realized, thinking of the slain guard. Shuddering, he closed his eyes. At least he'd prevented a horrible mistake from being made. Creatures such as this one needed to feed on human blood once each night to maintain their human appearance. It would have killed again and again, and kept on killing, as long as it dwelled among them.

* * * * *

The celebration was just winding down when Candabraxis returned. Harlmut glanced at the wizard as he staggered in. His ashen face and disheveled appearance spoke volumes.

"Excuse me," Harlmut said to Duke Leor, who was on his third pie of the evening, and rising, he hurried to the wizard's side.

"We must—talk alone—" the wizard gasped in a half-strangled whisper.

Harlmut hesitated, then gave a quick nod. Steadying the mage with one hand, he ushered him into his private office.

After seating Candabraxis in one of the chairs, Harlmut poured him a glass of wine, gave it to him, and watched impatiently as the wizard tried to swallow it, only to choke.

"What happened?" he said urgently.

"Orin Hawk . . ."

"He retired right before you did, remember?"

Candabraxis shook his head. "No . . . that wasn't Hawk, but a deadly creature that had taken his form."

"What?" Harlmut said with a gasp. "Where is Hawk, then? And where is this—this creature?"

The wizard held up his hand, gesturing for patience. "It's dead. I slew it. You see, Evann didn't bring back Orin Hawk at all. He brought back this undead creature, a bloodspawn—"

"A *what?*" Harlmut had never heard of such a creature before.

"A bloodspawn. They're very rare. I've heard of only one other instance in which they plagued men, and that was many years ago. They're a form of undead creature from the Shadow World. They take the appearance of men in order to move among them undetected, but they have to feed on blood each night to keep their form."

"How did it get in here?" he demanded. "I thought your spell protected the whole castle."

"He used this." Candabraxis opened his right hand. He held a talisman . . . one of the charms he'd made to protect Evann's men when they entered the Hag's Domain. "It allowed him to move freely through here, avoiding detection."

"Are there more of these *things* loose?"

"I don't think so. Have any more bloodless bodies turned up?"

"No . . ."

Candabraxis nodded. "Then we should be safe."

"But we don't have Orin Hawk."

"No. My guess is that he never left the Hag's Domain. The Hag figured out our plan, somehow, and made sure this creature returned with Evann instead."

Rising, Harlmut began to pace. This destroyed all his plans. Without Hawk, Drachenward would have no reason to help them. Without Drachenward, they had no hope of getting King Graben back. He felt a growing hollowness inside. He could have wept.

"At least one good thing has come of this," the wizard said softly. "You're rid of Bowspear."

Harlmut sighed. It was small enough consolation, he thought.

He poured himself a drink—brandy, this time— and downed it in one long swallow.

"I have to tell Duke Leor," he said. He wasn't looking forward to it.

* * * * *

To Leor, eating had become a subtle form of politics, another tool in his vast arsenal. It was amazing to him how much could be learned by sitting back in the course of a meal, watching those around you and listening while seemingly preoccupied with the food. Over the years he had discovered much valuable information that way.

When the wizard staggered in, looking half dead, his interests had instantly been aroused. He pretended to bury himself in a delightful boysenberry pie while he watched and listened.

Fifteen minutes after the wizard had been ushered by Harlmut into private chambers, the pair of them emerged, both looking gloomy. Bad news then, Leor thought. As they headed straight for him, he assumed it involved him in some way.

"Duke Leor," Harlmut said in a strangled voice,

"I'm afraid I have sad tidings."

He shifted his bulk around to face them. "Yes?"

"Orin Hawk . . ." He hesitated.

"An impostor?" Leor guessed, gently dabbing the corners of his mouth with a napkin.

"How did you know?" the wizard asked.

"A guess," he said. "One of the Hag's undead minions, perhaps?"

Harlmut nodded. "We just discovered it and destroyed it," he said.

Duke Leor only nodded. That made more sense, he thought. If the combined might of Drachenward had been unable to free Orin Hawk, it stood to reason that a small pirate kingdom like Grabentod had to fail on any such endeavor. At least this would save Drachenward the embarrassment of having to intercede with Müden on their behalf.

"I will leave with the morning tide," he said. "Now, if you'd be kind enough to pass that flagon of excellent Anuirean wine?"

Numbly, it seemed, Harlmut served him.

"Very kind of you," he said as he generously refilled his goblet. "An excellent feast, Regent Harlmut, I must say. Almost worth the trip itself."

"Thank you." Harlmut sank back in his chair, looking devastated.

And Leor, Duke of Drachenward, smiled in triumph.

ANUIRE

TWENTY-FIVE

From his tower suite, Candabraxis watched Duke Leor's ship sail. He sighed in disappointment. They had been so close to success. . . .

Shaking his head, he returned to his packing. He had decided to move on. The force that had drawn him to Grabentod seemed to have left him with the death of the bloodspawn, almost as if defeating it were the sole purpose of his coming here.

From his worktable, he lifted each jar and vial, carefully wrapped them in thick cloths, and stored them in his trunk. He would miss this tower. In the ew weeks he'd been here, it had become home.

A knock sounded on his door.

"Come in!" he called.

Harlmut stepped in. "I'm sorry to see you go," e said. "You are welcome to stay, Candabraxis. Ve do need a wizard."

Candabraxis grinned and shook his head. "The rge is on me to travel again, to see more of the vorld. I think my next stop will probably be Müden."

"Oh?" Harlmut raised his eyebrows.

The wizard laughed. "Yes, I'll stop in and see he Erbrecht family. Perhaps I can do some good or you after all . . . but I would not count on it. I vill, however, pass on any messages you care to ;ive me."

"Of course," Harlmut said.

"I will miss this place. And you, Regent. You're a ;ood man, and you deserve better than you've got- en. King Graben may not know how much you've lone for him . . . but I intend to let him know."

"When are you leaving?"

"Captain Evann said I could accompany him to- norrow. He's got word of a pair of Müden mer- hant ships passing by tomorrow night, on their eturn trip. After he's relieved them of their car- ;os, I'll book passage." He grinned. "I'm sure hey'll be happy to sail under a wizard's protec- ion the rest of the way."

Harlmut laughed, too. "I'll miss you, friend."

* * * * *

The next morning dawned gray. The breeze had come up, bringing a warmer southern wind, and the air tasted of rain to come.

Candabraxis watched the castle's porters carry his trunks aboard Captain Evann's roundboat They took exaggerated care with them, as though they contained priceless chinaware.

Captain Evann met him at the gangplank Evann had a haunted look and dark circles under his eyes.

"Please," he said softly, "I have to know . . . on the way back, one of my men died. He was little more than a boy, really, and he'd been badly wounded. Hawk—the creature, that is—tended him that night. I . . . need to know. Did it kill him?"

"Would your man have died anyway?" Candabraxis asked.

"I don't know. Probably. Maybe."

Candabraxis sighed. "Bloodspawn don't like to kill," he lied. "They prefer to take the freshly dead. If the boy was destined to die, the creature would have waited for his natural passing."

Evann looked relieved. "Thank you," he said.

"It's nothing."

Candabraxis crossed to the ship and moved to the bow, staring out across the waves. He'd thought his destiny might lie in Grabentod, but no. His future lay out there, somewhere to the south. Müden . . . or beyond? He couldn't say for sure. All he knew was that his wanderlust had returned, the itch that summoned him ever onward.

A soft rain began to fall. Glancing over his

shoulder at the castle, Candabraxis realized that without him there to repair it, the protective rune he had drawn would, in time, be slowly washed away.

Let it go, he thought. Somehow, whatever force had steered him here, whatever force had inspired him to protect the castle, had released him from its grip. He could only assume that Grabentod no longer needed such help.

...border at the Purple City, should realize that, without him, there were going to be problems and that he just might wind up in one. Especially a major one.

"... off he. I thought somehow, whatever you had rescued me... never left my eyes on each... next time to think they should have had no small merchant... guide we could make sure was that to standard on... I appreciated such help."

Aye, lad, ye heard right: one or two people have met the Hag and returned to tell of it. I know of fifty men who went after her gold, and only four of 'em came back. They were all strong men in their prime, and they turned up wandering the countryside, near witless for days. Seems she'd had her way with them, if ye know what I mean, and it drove 'em half crazy. Weren't none of 'em right in the head for months afterward.

So I reckon ye can get away from her, if ye're man enough to please her. Wouldn't want to try it myself, no sirree, not with this bum leg and a hook for a hand.

What more do I know of the Hag? Not much more, lad, not much more. Just that it's best to steer clear of her ports. Aye, and stick to the sea. The sea's a tricky enough lover herself, but ye can master her, given enough years.

Now that yer thoughts are turnin' to adventure, I'll put in a good word for ye with a captain friend of mine—never ye mind which one—and we'll see if we can't get ye a berth. Won't be much to start, but keep yer head down, follow orders, fight like a devil—and ye'll do good enough.

Now get home to your mother, lad, lest the Hag come for ye!

ANUIRE

εpiloque

At dawn, Wren unlatched the small shed and let loose her family's herd of seven goats. She'd take them to feed on the mountainside this morning, she decided. She knew of a small clearing where long yellow grass still stood. The goats had been there only twice so far this fall, and they would still find plenty to eat.

"Get up, there," she said, swatting old Gray-beard with her walking stick. He had hesitated and looked like he wanted to bolt in the wrong di-rection. She didn't want to spend the morning chasing him.

Bells jingling, the goats cooperated for once and set off in the right direction, across the empty fields covered with the stubble of mown hay. It was almost as if the goats smelled the grass waiting for them.

Wren followed. Her thoughts drifted to the coming harvest dance. Now that her father and brothers had brought in the last of the crops and mowed enough hay to last the winter, they could relax a little until the spring planting. Now that she was fourteen, time had come to start looking for a husband, and more and more her thoughts turned to Gunder Lann. He was fifteen, but unmarried yet, and certainly handsome enough . . . and he'd be at the harvest dance. . . .

At last she reached the clearing. The goats, drifting apart, began to eat.

Wren sat on a fallen log to watch. Herding goats could be frustrating sometimes and boring other times. Boring as long as she watched them, because they knew not to try any of their tricks, and frustrating because the moment her attention drifted, they would seize the opportunity to run off. She'd lost count of how many times she'd had to chase Graybeard across fields and forest, trying to catch him. No, she'd pay attention today, she thought.

The goats continued to graze, the little copper bells around their necks jingling now and again.

Suddenly a low moan interrupted the quiet.

Wren leapt to her feet and looked around. She

didn't see anyone. Who could have made that sound?

The moan came again, louder. It seemed to be coming from the trees behind her.

"Who's there?" she called, peering this way and that. She tightened her grip on her walking stick in case she had to defend herself. There shouldn't be anyone here, but in the edges of civilization all sorts of dangers lurked. Her parents had warned her often enough to watch her step. Although they'd never seen one, goblins were rumored to live in the mountains.

The moan came again. It sounded like someone hurt.

Wren hesitated. Then, with her walking stick upraised like a club, she slowly made her way into the trees.

Someone lay there, on the leaves . . . a man dressed in rags. His short black hair was matted and filthy, and he smelled of something indescribably foul.

"Who are you?" she demanded, nose wrinkling.

He turned his face toward her. His lips were thick and purplish. Blood and bruises marred his features, but she thought he might have been handsome once.

"Help me . . ." he gasped.

"Who are you?" she demanded again.

"Captain . . . Parniel . . . Bowspear . . ."

That seemed to be too much for him. He collapsed, eyes rolling back in his head. She could see that he was still breathing, though.

Wren hesitated, wondering what to do. Finally she took off her cloak and spread it over the stranger. He needed it more than she did right now. Then, whistling to the goats, she herded them back together and began the long trek down to her family's farm. Her father would know what to do, she thought.

* * * * *

"Phew, he stinks!" said a young man's voice.

"Don't he!" said another.

"Quiet there," a deeper voice said. "Get him up."

Bowspear felt strong hands lifting him. It hadn't been a dream or an hallucination, he realized. He really had seen that young woman. She really had gone for help.

He could barely breathe, barely move, but he managed to open his eyes. Farmers . . . four of them, a man and three boys who looked enough like him that they had to be his sons. Together they carried him to an ox-drawn cart and put him in the back. He closed his eyes as they covered him with blankets that smelled of horse sweat. Bowspear didn't mind. He just wanted to be warm again.

The rocking, jarring passage to their farm seemed to take forever. At last, though, they drove into a low barn and shut the doors. It was warmer in here, full of the smells of hay and animals.

With effort, Bowspear managed to sit up. They

brought an oil lamp and held it over him, looking him over as though he were a prize calf.

"Where you from?" the farmer said. "Wren said your name was Bowspear."

"Water . . ." he gasped.

One of the boys ran and fetched a small clay cup. He took it and drank deeply. Strengthened, he took a deep breath.

"I've been on a mission for King Graben," he said.

"The king, huh," the farmer scoffed. "The king's locked up in Müden. Don't you know that?"

Bowspear forced a laugh. "Of course I know it. We were supposed to free him . . ."

He launched into the tale of how he'd gone to help Captain Evann capture Orin Hawk from the Hag. It was half truth more than outright lie, and as he wove the tale, he saw their skepticism change to grudging belief to open admiration.

Yes, he thought, everyone would believe that tale when he got back to Alber. He'd have it well rehearsed by then, and with his men dead, no one could deny it. They probably thought him dead now. The mission had cost him a lot . . . but not everything. It would set his plans back. But one way or another he'd have Grabentod.

As he finished, Bowspear said, "It's winter. You won't have need of all your sons or your horses. . . . Lend me a horse and one of your boys to guide me back to Alber. I'll see that he returns safely with rewards aplenty for you and yours."

"Agreed," the farmer said quickly. "Jerron, Guntre, get a bath ready for Captain Bowspear. We'll get him cleaned up for his trip home."

Yes, Bowspear thought, sitting up. He'd be back in Alber in two days.

At least Evann had failed in his plan to kidnap Orin Hawk. He smiled faintly. Hawk had been with the Hag up until the moment she'd tired of Bowspear and kicked him from her bed. And without Hawk, King Graben wouldn't be coming back anytime soon. . . .

Or *ever*, if Bowspear had his way.

Appendix A

Letters from the archives of Oluvar Hawk,
regarding the disappearance of his son and heir,
Orin Hawk,
and the attempted rescue mission
headed by Tuan Reisser.

To His Excellency Lord Oluvar Hawk,
Greetings and Salutations!

I am dispatching this report with one of my trusted assistants, Jospar, in the hopes of his reaching you before first snowfall. The skies are gray and the air holds the promise of storms soon to come, so he will leave this very day. As I warned you, the mountain passes of the Hag's Domain may prove sufficient impediment to my travels that I may be forced to winter here. Luckily I foresaw this possibility, and our pack animals carry sufficient provisions to last until spring. My guards will, of course, supplement these rations with whatever game they can capture or kill. Do not worry, Lord Hawk, your investment in this expedition is safe. I have taken every precaution.

As yet, I have seen no sign of your son, or of the forty men under his command. As I advised you before I accepted your commission to find him and return him to Drachenward, I fear he may well be dead. There are sufficient dangers here, between the Hag, goblins, trolls, orogs, and even dragons. No communication of any kind from him probably means he has been set upon by one or more such dangers. At the very least, however, I will return his body to you for proper burial.

Most fortuitously, I have made contact with a few humans who live close by my present camp. They report that the Hag has not been seen in some years by them. I find this news encouraging. Since their village of Merkstadt appears prosperous and healthy, and their lands appear rich and fertile, I can only assume they have lived here in relative safety for some years. It seems the Hag's reputation may well be exaggerated in Drachenward, if indeed she still exists.

Allow me to begin, however, with our journey. My course through the Drachenaur Mountains was uneventful. We sighted one dragon in the distance—a small creature, really, as such things are reckoned—but it paid us no heed. We also came upon the bones of a large troll, but the monster had been dead for some years, probably killed by brave adventurers from Drachenward, perhaps even your own relatives. I know the Hawk family has a well-deserved reputation for such noble deeds. Here is another that can surely be ascribed to them.

Upon gaining access to the plain at the center of the Hag's Domain, I followed a series of streams until I came to a settlement of perhaps fifty small stone houses. Clearly, I realized, this settlement had been in place for some time. The cottages looked well tended. Fields for many acres around the village had been cleared, and although the crops had all been harvested, everything spoke of a small happy little community.

(One parenthetical note: should Drachenward choose to exert its rightful claim over Merkstadt and its inhabitants, force may be necessary. I estimate their potential military strength at approximately sixty-five men of military age. Although I have seen no swords, I suspect the villagers are well armed and may fight fiercely to protect their perceived freedom. Their houses certainly seem strong and well fortified.)

I have made subtle inquiries about their origins. It seems they are descended of refugees from barbaric Grabentod—people of the court who fled when the pirate-king, Ulrich Graben, seized the throne some years ago. They fled here and founded Merkstadt, which has prospered ever since.

Despite their rough origins and the history of enmity between Drachenward and Grabentod, these people seem friendly enough to me and my companions. I plan to use Merkstadt as the base for all expeditions deeper into the Hag's Domain over the coming months, as weather permits. I will attempt to send communications through to you as often as I have information.

If you could send an additional five fighting men with Jospar, it would prove helpful. Five of my men were lost when part of the pass upon which they walked fell away into a deep abyss. Although I can doubtless accomplish my task with the eighteen men I have left, reinforcements would speed the matter.

You may send any new messages or instructions back to me through Jospar. He is a hearty mountaineer, and I trust in his ability to make it through the pass to rejoin me.

Your humble servant,
Tuan Reisser

To His Excellency, Lord Oluvar Hawk,
Greetings and Salutations!

Many thanks for sending the additional men I requested. Unfortunately, only one of them made it through the pass with Jospar—they were set upon by a troll, which killed four before itself being mortally wounded.

Despite that, I am pleased to report some small success in my investigations. I have found definitive proof that your son and his men did, in fact, make it through the mountains and into the Hag's Domain. (Truly, after my friendly reception in Merkstadt, I had begun to suspect young Orin might have been waylaid by goblins and dragged with his men into the maze of tunnels rumored to exist beneath the Drachenaur mountains.) So, surely, this must be seen as good news.

Along with Jospar, I am returning for your review the helm of a Drachenwarder light infantryman. I believe the insignia marks it as belonging to the Fourth Regiment, which your son commanded.

Please note that the helm bears no marks other than a little rust and tarnish from being exposed to the elements. I take this as a sign that it was inadvertently lost in packing up camp, rather than in the midst of battle. We saw no other signs of Orin Hawk or his men, however—no broken weapons, no bones, not even a fire ring for a camp.

I will concentrate my search for now in this area. Of course, as soon as I have more news, I will advise you at once. Although snow has fallen in the mountains, Jospar reports that the pass remains clear enough for travel, at least for the present time. More men will make the search proceed faster. If you have another five to spare, please send them with Jospar, along with any other messages or instructions.

Your humble servant,
Tuan Reisser

To His Excellency Lord Oluvar Hawk,

Once again I have good news. Your additional ten men reached me in good health and high spirits. Our search for your son continues apace.

We met a wandering trader who claims the Hag died about five years ago, when an avalanche buried the cave in which she kept her lair. Though I have no confirmation of this, I suspect it must be true, for we have seen no sign of her or her minions. This trader reports your son is not only living and in good health, but happily married in another village close to the Grabentod border.

It seems young Orin Hawk killed a local robber-baron and has proclaimed himself king of the Hag's Domain. If the trader's tale is correct, he is busy uniting all the disparate villages under his own enlightened rule, using his forty infantrymen as an army. Apparently he is conquering everything and everyone in his path. Within a year, according to the trader, he will be ruler of a kingdom nearly as large and prosperous as Grabentod.

I am heading for that village tomorrow morning. If you have any instructions or messages, please give them to Jospar at once. We expect more snow in the mountain passes soon, and he must hurry if he is going to return here before the spring.

I will investigate further and relay information to you as quickly as I can.

Your humble servant,
Tuan Reisser

Greetings and Salutations, Lord Hawk—

This unseasonable thaw will doubtless allow Jospar to reach you once again. And, once again, I report good news—I have met with your son and find him fit and well, although somewhat thin and worn. I am enclosing a letter from him to you, which will, I think, explain matters more fully.

I pray you, pay no attention to the reports of the Hag's continued influence in Drachenward. She is quite clearly dead; your son has confirmed this, since he has recovered her body and laid it to rest, abomination that she was. As I am certain you already know, it is very easy to blame any and all strange occurrences on the nearest awnshegh. If the Hag caused every stillbirth and pox and pimple in Drachenward, what time would she have to rule her own lands? Feh, by Sera, it is all silly superstition.

I plan on spending the rest of the winter here, then returning to Drachenward to receive the balance of my payment. I will see you at that time.

I remain,

> Your humble and obedient servant,
> Tuan Reisser

Honored Father—

Yes, this letter is truly from me, Orin. You must surely recognize my seal and my handwriting, Father, if not my voice in these words.

All that Tuan Reisser has written you is true. The Hag is dead. I saw an opportunity here and have taken it for the greater glory of our family.

My forces now occupy roughly half of what was once the Hag's Domain (and which I now call Hawksward). I will rule it all by summer, with your help. Then, together, we can rule a new country that will last unto the final days of Cerilia herself!

For now, I must keep Tuan Reisser and all the men you have sent with him here. I fear retribution from our cousin, the king of Drachenward. We are not yet in a position of strength, should he wish to add us to his kingdom. I pray you, do not breathe a word of this letter to anyone yet.

The people here are simple and prosperous, but steadfast in their love of freedom and independence. It is only by the sword and the lance that they submit to my rule. If you would help me, if you would see me succeed in this mission, send as many more men as you can spare. What I need most now are fighters able to back my claim to these lands.

Your devoted son,
Orin

Honored Father—

The additional twenty-two men have arrived. Unfortunately, I need still more. I realize you are taxing your own reserves to their limit, but I urge you to do whatever you can to support me in this measure. My forces are spread far too thinly here to maintain order while still expanding my reach. I beseech you to help me to your limits.

Your devoted son,
Orin

Honored Father—

I am bewildered by your refusal to send additional men. I am surrounded by enemies on every side. We have encountered goblins in the mountains as well as trolls. Murmurs of discontent are spreading among the conquered villages. I have attempted to levy troops from them with little success.

The only way to insure my safety is to conquer before I am conquered. Please, why won't you help? Another twenty men will suffice for now. Think not of yourself, but of the future of our family.

Yes, as I wrote you earlier, the Hag is dead. I saw her body myself. These continuing stories of her meddling in Drachenward are false. Pay them no heed.

This spring, after the thaw, you and Mother must visit me here. My castle is progressing nicely. I have found several capable masons among the villagers, and I am putting their talents to good use.

Your devoted son,
Orin

Father—

I am dismayed that you and Mother have no plans to visit me here this spring. Or ever. You would have made very welcome visitors. Your decision to send no more men to aid me is also troublesome, as well as your request to return the ones already sent. Yes, I know they have been here for six months, but their work is not yet done.

As you seem to have guessed, the Hag does indeed still live. My apologies for deceiving you, Father, but it was necessary. She is a most wonderful mistress. Her commands are wise and insightful. You and Mother would love her, if you met her. I plan to marry her at the first opportunity, so great is my love. She will bear you many fine grandchildren, I'm certain.

All of our men love her, too, and grow likewise more devoted to her with each passing day. She is beautiful.

I have agreed to guard her borders. Make no more attempts to rescue me or the men under my command (even those who were yours). We all serve our new mistress willingly, and will do so to our dying day.

If, on the other hand, you change your mind, you would be honored guests here. Please, do visit us. The Hag's Domain has vast game lands where we could hunt together as we did in the days of my youth.

You ask of Tuan Reisser. Do not think to send more men like him to "rescue" me. He died shortly after he arrived, and, undead, he penned his letters to you. We have since laid him to rest. Poor loyal servant, nothing the Hag could do would persuade him to love her, like I love her.

Your devoted son,
Orin

ANUIRE

appendix B

*Letters from Lan Harlmut, Regent of Grabentod,
to His Royal Majesty King Graben, in Müden.*

Your Majesty,

I am saddened to report the loss of the wizard
Ythril Candabraxis, whom as you may recall from
my last letter had taken up residence in the east
tower of Castle Graben. I find I do not blame him,
for he was sorely treated here, attacked first by
Parniel Bowspear while at sea on a ship bound for
Müden, then nearly murdered by an assassin sent
by (I suspect) Haltengabben, then almost drained
of blood by an undead creature under the Hag's
control.

I have continued my inquiries into obtaining the
services of another wizard. Perhaps word of Candabraxis's reception will not spread quickly.

Candabraxis, who remained helpful and receptive until the very moment of his departure, gave
me the name of his old master in Suiriene, Razlev,
and suggested I contact him with an eye toward
placing one of his journeymen in your employ.
Doubtless such an endeavor will prove expensive.
Nevertheless, with Parniel Bowspear gone—and
hopefully dead—my attentions can once more
turn to the future of your kingdom. If nothing else,
spoils are good this season.

Have faith, my lord and king. You will live to
see the open skies of Grabentod over your head
once more.

Your servant,
Lan Harlmut, Regent

Your Majesty,

I must regretfully report the survival of Parniel Bowspear. He staged a less-than-impressive return this morning, trundled (as he was) into Alber aboard an ox cart. It seems a farmer near the Drachenaur Mountains found him wandering, filthy and near death, and nursed him back to health. He meant well.

All the men whom Bowspear took with him are dead. Eaten by goblins, it seems. Bowspear seems to be winning some public sympathy for his ordeal, but little actual support. Most generally accept his story of leading a secret mission to help Captain Evann, but of course his spectacular failure is quite plain.

Evann remains hero of the hour. Despite his ultimate lack of success, he did manage to lead his men safely back, which is more than Bowspear can say.

For now, we seem to have an uneasy truce among all the political factions in Alber. I suspect Bowspear will soon try to build up support again, and his ambitions will surely drive him toward your throne. However, that time still lies far in the future. Bowspear will need to rebuild his alliances, gather new men, and bide his time—which will take years.

You will be on your throne again well before then, Sire.

Your servant,
Lan Harlmut, Regent

appendix c

*Letters from Ythril Candabraxis, wizard,
to Razlev, his former master,
concerning events in Grabentod.*

Greeting, Razlev, whom I once called Master—

You had requested periodic letters concerning my travels as I sought a place in the world for myself. I realize this will be only my second such update, and that it follows close upon the last, but I feel obliged to write you at once because I feel I owe my life to your teachings.

I had not realized it at the time, but your philosophy of forcing the individual to take responsibility toward defeating evil, in whatever form it takes, is correct. I encountered an undead creature in Grabentod which attempted to kill me in order to feed on my blood. It was only through calm rational thought that I managed to thwart its plans.

Its defeat forced my thoughts toward a greater picture of the world, one in which good and evil are more than mere abstractions, but equal and opposite forces constantly at war, pushing at each other. I doubt if either can completely conquer the other, for there is a balance in such things, but I now see the need to work tirelessly toward maintaining that balance.

Evil could have overwhelmed Grabentod. It was only through my chance presence that good (if it is possible to categorize pirates and their culture as good) managed to win out.

So, my old Master, I thank you yet again.

I remain,

Your student,
Ythril Candabraxis

Greeting, Razlev, whom I once called Master—

I find myself in Müden, which is an amazing, bustling city like none I have ever seen before. So many ships are docked here I could not count them all. The port bustles at all hours of the day, and ten thousand warehouses hold the goods of a hundred-score merchant princes. I have never seen such wealth in my life.

Nor have I ever seen such poverty.

Just as I last wrote you saying that good and evil mirror one another, so too do wealth and poverty. The rich here continue to prosper, and the poor barely have enough to eat. I have dined with several rich merchants and their families, and the leftovers from their smallest meal would feed a family of ten for a week. Such scraps, however, are given to pets.

I followed up on my promise to Harlmut, Regent of Grabentod, to visit King Graben. He is an enormously fat man living in a prison such as you or I would call a palace. He is surrounded by the finest of everything—silks, furs, jewels, women—and wants for nothing. He dines nightly with merchants and their noble-born visitors. If chains he has, they are silken.

I feel no doubt that he could escape, and easily, if he so chose. However, life here is so comfortable, why should he? He lives better than he did in his own castle. Poor Harlmut—I grieve for him and his people. Perhaps they would be better with someone like Parniel Bowspear as their king.

I have decided to write none of this to Harlmut, however. It might serve to discourage him. He is a good man, and very loyal to his king. Alas, he no longer has a king worthy of such loyalty.

I have decided to press on from here. I have found a merchant willing to take me as a passenger to Anuire, where he plans to trade for wines. (His cargo will be furs and silks.) As soon as I arrive, I will write you again.

The pull of adventure calls me, and I feel my destiny may, in fact, lie in Anuire. As I listen to the way the name rolls from my tongue, my mind conjures images of decadent ports, ancient cities, and mysteries to be unraveled. I long to explore the unknown.

I remain,

Your student,
Ythril Candabraxis

An Excerpt

War

Simon Hawke

Now Availale in Hardcover from

ANUIRE

prologue

The stench of death on the evening breeze was
overpowering. There was a thrumming in the air
from the buzzing of the flies, thousands of them,
swarming over the bloody corpses on the battlefield as the sun slowly sank behind the mountains.
Katrina lifted her riding skirt as she walked
among the broken bodies littering the churned–up
ground, looking to see if she could recognize any
of them.

There was Cedric, the archer, who had taught
her to shoot when she was a little girl and neither

of her brothers would agree to show her how, because they said it wasn't ladylike. Dark blood matted his thick gray beard as he lay sprawled out on the ground, eyes and mouth open, flies clustered on his gaping wounds. One arm still held his crossbow, but the arm was no longer attached to his body. It lay beside him, hacked off, on a patch of bare ground dark with all the blood that had soaked in. And there, just a few yards beyond, was Gavilan, captain of the horse guard, who had helped her train her first colt. He would never ride again. Unhorsed by a spear that still transfixed him, the sharp angle giving testimony to how it had been thrust upward by a foot soldier. The spear had caught Gavilan in a vulnerable spot just beneath the arm, where he had no armor to protect him. He had probably raised his sword to bring it down on his antagonist, who had been lucky enough to strike first.

Katrina could almost picture it, how the spear had been thrust upward just as Gavilan had raised his blade and leaned down from the saddle, his momentum as he rode helping drive the iron tip right through his coat of mail as the spearman braced against the ground. A fluke. The spearman might easily have missed and struck the breastplate; the tip would have glanced off; the shaft might have been snapped. The odds of getting it just right, maintaining balance as the spear ripped through the mail and passed into the chest . . . Gavilan must have been dead before he hit the ground. His helm was open, with just the steel nasal jutting down between his eyes, which were open and staring blankly at the sky.

I should be horrified, thought Katrina. I should be in tears. My body should be racked with sobs, as Mother's was when they brought Father home. I should be feeling . . . something.

Instead, she just felt numb. She walked like a somnambulist among the carnage, the cool breeze ruffling her long red hair as the sun set slowly behind the mountains. It was as if she were somehow apart from herself, in the middle of it all, yet at the same time disconnected from it.

Katrina paused as she spotted Branmor's crest on a white tabard soaked with blood. Tall and handsome, blond and blue-eyed Branmor, who had danced with her not two weeks earlier at the feast held in honor of Lady Lydia's sixteenth birthday. Katrina had reveled in the jealous looks she got from the other young ladies of the court as she and Branmor led the promenade, his eyes never leaving her as they danced. His visored helm had been split by a powerful blow from a short battleaxe, and Katrina was grateful she could not see his face. The blade of the axe had cut through almost to the collarbone and was still embedded there grotesquely. Somehow, despite the graphic evidence, it did not look real.

None of it looked real. The scene was like a frozen image from some nightmare. Many of the bodies were draped over one another, as if they had been dumped there from a loaded charnel wagon. And too many had faces that she knew.

Some had no faces left at all. She had to pick her footing carefully as she walked among them. Had she wanted to, she could have crossed the battlefield without ever setting foot upon the ground, just by stepping from corpse to corpse to corpse.

Katrina had never seen a dead body before. She had always been sheltered from such things. Now, she was surrounded by hundreds of them, strewn across the battlefield like discarded dolls. Unnaturally stiff and already bloating from hours of lying in the open under the summer sun. The battle had taken place that morning between the forces of Derwyn of Boeruine and Kier of Avan, two of the most powerful dukes in the crumbling empire, and this was the grisly aftermath of their ambition. Nothing had been settled. Each wanted to sit upon the Iron Throne now that the emperor was dead, slain by the Gorgon with no heir to take his place. Each commanded armies that had met in battle after fighting a number of small skirmishes designed to test the other's borders. And each had retired with what forces they had left when it became apparent that if they continued, their armies would simply slaughter one another. No clear victory for either side was in the offing.

Neither of them could afford to sustain extremely heavy losses. A few hundred men here and there could be replaced eventually, but greater losses would leave them undermanned and vulnerable, at least in the short term, to attack by any of the dozen or more other aspirants to the Anuirean crown. So they had prudently withdrawn to fight another day. And all these men had died, essentially, for nothing.

So this was war, thought Katrina.

She tried to imagine what it must have been like in the heat of battle, with men sweltering in some sixty pounds of armor and grunting with exertion as they fought, while the morning sun rose higher and the choking dust raised by all the churning feet and hooves coated their parched throats, already raw from screaming. She could almost hear the din, the cacophonous clangor of the blades, the neighing of the horses, the shouts of the commanders, the cries of the wounded and dying, all blending together like the howling of some gigantic and terrifying beast.

Thank the gods that I am not a man, she thought.

Her father had been brought home on a stretcher, and if he managed to survive his wounds, the physic said he would be crippled. Her brothers had not come home at all. Both of them were lying out here somewhere. She had come out to look for them, but now she didn't want to find them. She had thought, perhaps, if they were wounded . . . but there was no sound on the battlefield at all. No moans. No cries. Nothing. Just an eerie stillness.

And the buzzing of the flies.

"Terrible, is it not?" a low voice said from behind her. A woman's voice. Katrina turned.

Standing a short distance away was a figure dressed in a dark, woolen cloak with a hood covering her head. The cloak came down to her ankles and she carried a long wooden staff. The hood kept her features in shadow, so Katrina couldn't make them out. In the twilight, she saw only darkness where the face should be. A shiver passed through her. It was as if Death were standing there, looking out over its melancholy domain.

But this figure was flesh and blood, a woman like herself. Doubtless, Katrina thought, this woman had come out to the battlefield in search of fallen kin, just as Katrina had. As the woman approached, Katrina could make out strands of long blonde hair escaping from under her hood. As she came closer still, Katrina could see how beautiful the woman truly was. Her features were fine and delicate; her skin, like porcelain. She looked young, but there was something about her gaze that did not speak at all of youth.

"Terrible," the woman repeated as she gazed out across the battlefield, "and yet, at the same time, magnificent."

"Magnificent?" said Katrina, astonished at the comment, so bizarre and inappropriate.

"Indeed," the woman said, her gaze sweeping the awful scene around them. Her voice was throaty and sensual. "Do you not find it so? Does it not overwhelm you? Does it not seize you with its terrible majesty? Is it not almost more than your senses can encompass?"

"Yes," said Katrina, following her gaze. "Yes, I suppose it is, when you put it that way."

"There are few things in this world that can be

so magnificent and terrible as war," the woman said, still gazing at the battlefield as the shadows lengthened. "It represents man in his true element, enacting nature's endless drama, the survival of the fittest." She turned to Katrina. "Have you ever seen two colonies of ants at war?"

Katrina shook her head.

The woman smiled. "Well, perhaps you have and simply didn't pay attention. Boys are much more apt to notice such things. They will stop and stare for hours, enraptured by the struggle. Two tiny armies, each as organized as any that men could ever field, even more so, if truth be told. Locked in their grim struggle, one force attacking, one defending, they will fight for hours, sometimes even days, oblivious to any small boy who stops to watch them. And inevitably, when that boy grows tired of the spectacle, he will kick over the anthill and stamp upon the ants . . . without even really knowing why. Then he grows up to be a man, and joins an army, and becomes caught up in the same struggle. And regardless of whatever else he may have managed to accomplish in his life, war reduces him to the same size as that ant. And the gods look down and watch, just as that small boy once did. There is an irony in that, and a clue to the mystery of life."

"I never thought of it that way before," said Katrina, turning to look out across the darkening battlefield. "You make it sound so bleak . . . so pointless."

"Life is pointless, if it is merely lived," the

woman said. "There are forces acting upon all of us. The point is in knowing what they are and understanding them, then making the best use of that knowledge, so that one lives in tune with those forces, rather than in discord."

"How?" asked Katrina.

"Take hold of my staff," the woman told her.

Katrina looked puzzled, but did as the woman said. No sooner had her fingers touched the staff than she felt them start to tingle. The tingling sensation quickly passed up along her arm and spread throughout her body. She trembled, but it was not from the evening chill. Her fingers couldn't seem to let go of the staff.

"Now, look around and tell me what you see," the woman said. Her voice sounded distant, even though they were standing right beside each other.

"I see waste," said Katrina, slowly. "I see a battle that was fought between two forces, evenly matched. A battle in which nothing was resolved. So it is a battle which must be fought again. And there shall be other battles just like this one, between other forces, all competing for the crown. Each trying to dominate the other. And it shall go on . . . and on . . . and on."

The woman nodded. "And is there no way to break the cycle?"

"Not until one is stronger than the other," Katrina said, trembling as she held the staff. It seemed as if some sort of energy were flowing through it and passing into her. "Strong enough to stand against all others who would stake their claim to rule the empire."

"And how might that be accomplished?" asked the woman.

"If the two strongest contenders were to unite," said Katrina, "then none of the others, individually, could stand against them. Not unless alliances were formed. And one alliance would lead to others as the weaker parties joined their forces to defend against the stronger. And those left out would seek to ally themselves with the contender they deemed to be the strongest, with the best chance of victory in the end. And in this way, the empire would one day be reunited."

She was amazed at how clearly she could see it. She understood now. The ebb and flow of power, alignments and realignments, the politics of struggle and survival. It would not happen overnight, but it was inevitable. It was the way of things. Such were the forces which controlled these men, who had died here on the battlefield, caught in an inexorable tide of events that none of them had been able to resist. And she, too, had been caught up in the flow, her father crippled, perhaps dead by now, her brothers slain. . . . Now there would be no one to care for her or for her mother.

The sudden realization came upon her with a shock. What was she to do? How would they live? Her mother was no longer young. If no man were to take them in, what would become of them? It shall be up to me, thought Katrina. She was young enough and pretty enough to attract any number of men of means and position. Branmor had not been the first to show an interest, and she knew how jealous many of the other girls had been when he had started to pay court to her. But where was Branmor now? A handsome and promising young knight, a favorite of Avan's, now he lay dead with all the others, rendered equal in standing at the last with the lowliest man-at-arms. And with the coming wars, the risk would be the same for any other man. Unless, perhaps . . .

" 'Allo, my lady!"

Katrina jerked, startled out of her reverie. She closed her fingers on empty air. The staff was gone. So was the woman in the hooded cloak, as if she had never been there at all. Katrina turned, disoriented and confused.

Several riders were approaching at a walk. She turned to run, then realized she would never be able to outdistance them. What had happened to the woman in the cloak? There was no sign of her on the open field. Katrina scanned the bodies around her on the ground, thinking perhaps her companion had seen the riders and was trying to conceal herself among the dead. . . . But no, she was nowhere to be seen. Katrina turned back to face the approaching riders.

"This is no place for a woman, my lady," one of them said, coming to a halt before her. He wore a dark tabard with a crest she was unfamiliar with over a suit of mail. Perhaps he wore a breastplate under the tabard, but he was not in full armor. Nor were any of his companions. "It grows dark," he said. "The dogrobbers will be coming out soon with their torches, to strip the bodies of the fallen and gather such booty as they may." He cast an appreciative gaze over her. "It is not safe for you to be here."

"No, I imagine not," she replied. "But do I have more to fear from the dogrobbers than from you?"

The knight smiled. "The dogrobbers are likely to be somewhat less chivalrous."

"Well, if I am to be raped and taken, then by all means, let it be done chivalrously," she replied.

The knight chuckled. "You hear that?" he said, glancing over his shoulder at his companions, who shared his amusement. "A riposte of wit, and in such surroundings as these, no less." He turned back to her and bowed from the saddle. "My compliments, my lady. But I know you not. Are you of Avan or Boeruine?"

Not Avanil, she thought, but Avan. The province of Boeruine bore the same name as the family which governed it, but the duke of Avan's holding was called Avanil. He was asking if she was for Kier of Avan or Derwyn of Boeruine. Such was the new way of things, she thought. Not where are you from, but to whom do you owe fealty?

"My father and my brothers fought for Kier of Avan," she replied.

"So?" the knight said. He glanced back at his companions. "It seems we are confronted by the enemy." They grinned. He turned back to Katrina. "And how fared your kin on this day?"

"My two brothers lie here somewhere, slain,"

she replied flatly. "My father was still alive when last I saw him, but he was maimed, and the physic said that he may not survive."

The knight nodded. His companions looked grim. "I am sorry for your loss," he said sincerely. "It would seem that you have far more reason to despise Derwyn of Boeruine than ties of vassalage alone."

"If I were to despise Boeruine," she said, "then I would have just reason to despise the Duke of Avanil as well, for each played an equal part in this. Yet, did either really have a choice? Or were they merely playthings of the gods, pieces moved about in their never-ending game? Do I despise Boeruine? I think, if I were to despise anyone, it would be the emperor for getting himself killed in a lost and foolish cause, leaving the Iron Throne without an heir to sit upon it."

"What is your name, my lady?" asked the knight.

"Katrina of Tremayne."

"Lord Derek Tremayne's house?"

"My father," Katrina said.

The knight nodded. "I know of him. A goodly knight, by all accounts. I am Derwyn of Boeruine."

Katrina's eyes widened and she swallowed hard. She curtsied, as much to mask her reaction as out of courtesy. "Forgive me, my lord," she said. "Had I known who you were, I should not have addressed you in so familiar a manner."

"I did not take exception," Derwyn replied easily. "You shall enjoy the hospitality of my tent tonight. It would not be safe for a beautiful young woman to go riding back alone after dark."

"And if I were to refuse, my lord?"

"You need have no fear for your virtue," Derwyn assured her. "You have my knightly word on that. In the meantime, we shall send a messenger for word of your father. Bors, fetch the lady's horse."

In the distance, she could already see the flickering torches of the dogrobbers as they made their way onto the battlefield. Darkness cloaked the bodies lying all around her, rendering them as indistinct lumps upon the ground. Soon to be stripped bare by the dogrobbers, she thought, disgusted. But then they too were merely trying to survive.

Her thoughts turned back to that strange woman who had vanished as suddenly as she had appeared. Was she truly flesh and blood, as she had seemed, or had she been a spirit? Or was she a sorceress? That staff . . . She could still feel its power coursing through her. And Katrina knew that, somehow, she had changed.

As the knight named Bors brought up her horse, she allowed him to assist her into the saddle, then glanced at the duke. So you rode out from your camp tonight to see your handiwork, she thought. Does it satisfy your lordship? Are you proud?

He was regarding her curiously. She thought, do you like what you see? And how good is your knightly word to vouchsafe my virtue? Who is to say nay to you should you decide to break it? He raised his eyebrows at her scrutiny and she lowered her gaze demurely. "I thank you for your kindness and your chivalry, my lord," she said, softly. "You honor me."

"The honor is mine, my lady," Derwyn replied, bowing slightly from the saddle.

She recalled hearing that he was a widower. His late duchess, the Princess Laera, had given him a son, the Baron Aerin, who stood next in line to inherit not only his father's title, but quite possibly the throne as well, by dint of his descent from the Emperor Michael's bloodline. However, there were many who disputed his legitimacy. Michael Roele had six other sisters, all of whom had married various nobles and produced offspring of their own, and since Laera's death, dozens of men had come forward—from young noblemen to men-at-arms and stableboys—all claiming to have been her lovers. The treacherous part that she had played in the death of the Empress Faelina, to say nothing of her evil sorcery, had made Princess Laera the most hated and reviled woman in the empire. She had brought disgrace down on the House of Boeruine, and word had it that Lord Derwyn would not even permit her name to be mentioned in his presence.

Katrina wondered how Lord Derwyn managed to justify his son's claim to the throne if he could not even mention the name of Aerin's mother. And she wondered how Aerin felt about it all. Accusations against Princess Laera were countered by accusations from supporters of Lord Derwyn that her sisters—or their husbands—had bribed the men who had come forward to give testimony to Laera's numerous infidelities. Lord Derwyn was either the victim of vicious political intrigues or else he was the greatest cuckold in the empire. Quite possibly both, Katrina thought.

The Baron Aerin would not be at the camp, if the stories she had heard were true. It was said that Lord Derwyn was very protective of his son, through whom he laid his much-disputed claim to regency. Derwyn feared conspiracies and the possibility that harm might come to Aerin, thereby nullifying his claim. Baron Aerin was thirty-one years old and had never even seen a battlefield. It was said that he had never fought in tournament or, some said, even held a sword. He was kept cloistered within the walls of Seaharrow, Lord Derwyn's impregnable castle on a rocky bluff overlooking the Miere Rhuann, guarded like a rare and precious jewel. What must it be like, Katrina wondered, to live a life like that? And how must Aerin feel about a father who keeps him practically prisoner?

She glanced at Lord Derwyn as they rode back toward his camp. He was not a young man, perhaps in his midfifties, yet he still looked very fit and handsome. His face bore the lines of age and his hair was white, but his vitality was clearly evident in the brightness of his eyes and the alertness of his gaze. His voice was deep and rich, and he possessed all the courtly graces, but his chin was weak and there was a softness about his features.

It was said that Laera, while she lived, had kept him firmly under her thumb. A man who could be controlled, by the right woman. And he had never remarried.

He sent Bors to Avanil to find out how her father fared. A chivalrous gesture, to be sure. And, under the circumstances, Lord Kier would be sure to give Sir Bors safe-conduct. But the physic's words came back to Katrina, as he had spoken them to her outside her father's chamber, where her mother waited, weeping, by his bedside. "I shall not lie to you, my lady. The truth is that I fear your father shall not see the dawn."

My two brothers dead in battle and my father dying, thought Katrina. And here am I, found wandering on the battlefield amid the corpses, angered, shocked, and numb with horror. . . . Who would blame a woman for succumbing to her grief in such deeply tragic circumstances? Who would blame her for turning to a strong man for comfort and solace?

How long has it been, she wondered, since Lord Derwyn had a woman?

More...

from

The Abominations

The Vault
by Bruce L. Nakaone

...Richard Archer ... ...used ... a few
... of land for ... Farm ... but instead
found ... ...house ... with ... and
a winged ... Dare! ... ...between King himself
... ...

The New Throne
by Simon Hawke

The Serpent — the most powerful and most evil
... of all the wizards of Conru — ...himself for the
final ... of ... Michael Roque himself.

...and the living ...

OWLFLIGHT
by Anne McCaffrey

When he went to the Sudden World opens in
the event ... slowly as the sun of the ever-
rest in his ... of a lonely ... forced to
flee, out ... all by ...

Threescore generations have passed since that impossible day when six gods sacrificed themselves to destroy one of their own and the bloodlines were born.

Mount Deismaar
Cerilia, Year Zero

The human tribes—my ancestors—moved up into the wilderness of Cerilia from the southern continent of Aduria, dragging their gods with them. Crossing a land bridge now hidden deep under the waves of the Straits of Aerele, they found seemingly limitless land in which to grow and prosper. So, too, did they find desperate enemies and the evil agents of the very god from whom they fled—the Shadow, Azrai.

Years of war and bloodshed followed, and Azrai gained in followers among those seeking to protect their ancestral lands. The Shadow made converts even among the reclusive elves, who first welcomed the newcomers to Cerilia, but soon grew wary of their expansion. As dark forces grew to both the north and south, the human tribes were forced together and went to war as allies in the War of Shadow.

Like their human followers, Anduiras, god of war and nobility; Reynir, goddess of the woods and streams; Brenna, goddess of commerce and fortune; Vorynn, lord of the moon and magic;

Masela, the lady of the seas; and Basaïa, queen of the sun, joined the fight against the Shadow, Azrai. Lines were drawn, champions chosen . . . blood spilled.

Until they all came to face each other at the foot of Mount Deismaar. Those who survived did not have words to describe the explosive burst of energy—the power no mortal should ever have been exposed to—and the mountain was gone. With it, to oblivion, went Azrai and the other gods—all of them. Six destroyed themselves to destroy one, for the sake of millions of suffering mortals and the future of Cerilia.

But what happens when man and elf, goblin and dwarf are showered with the essence of the gods? This instant of destruction became an instant of creation, and the bloodlines of Cerilia were born. Some, bathed in the glory of the likes of Anduiras, became great heroes, champions of justice. Others, corrupted by the malignant power of Azrai, became hideous monsters, abominations—*awnsheghlien*.

A dozen years of chaos passed in the wake of Deismaar. The champions of the dead gods, now possessed of supernatural powers of their own, fed on the empowered blood of the other survivors in the brutal practice of *bloodtheft*. From this chaos, the Empire of Anuire was born and some measure of peace came to Cerilia.

Then, like all things, the Anuirean Empire came to an end. Some say the true spirit of the empire never really survived the death of its founder,

Michael Roele, less than half a century after his rise to power. Still, what remained of the empire held sway over Cerilia for nearly a millennium, and then was gone. On the ruins of the empire grew the beginnings of the Cerilian kingdoms of today, our own among them. Led by the descendants of the survivors of Deismaar, these kingdoms hold the future of Cerilia in their unsteady hands.

Who will be the next Roele?

What will be the next Anuire . . . the next Deismaar?

We, the people of Cerilia, tempered by our unimaginable past, look toward our future with fear . . . and with hope.

—Rhobher Nichaleir
Archprelate of the Western Imperial Temple, Tuornen